Dark Thunder

By

Robyn Braemer

Halstad House

Dark Thunder

By Robyn Braemer

Copyright © 2013 by Robyn Braemer

Published by Halstad House

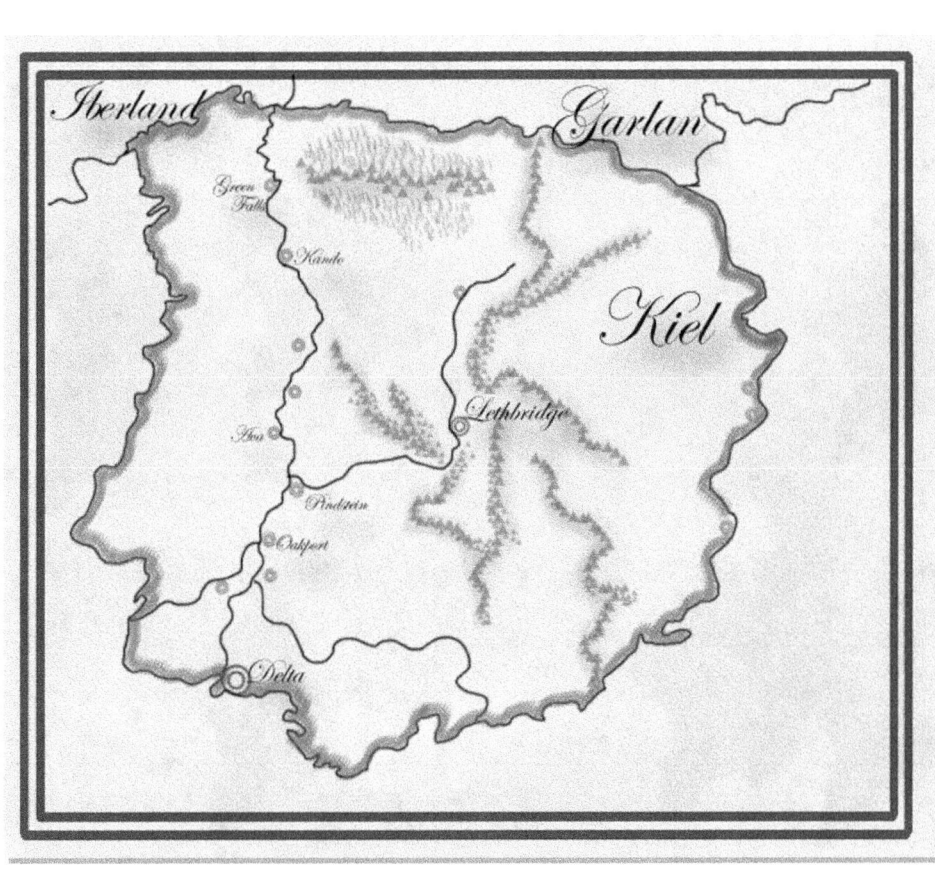

Chapter One

The wagon rumbled down from hill country onto the plains. It was an over-sized, wooden monstrosity, a house on wheels pulled by three horses in tandem. The horses' harness jingled with the movement of iron-shod hooves stepping briskly along the rutted dirt road. The wheels squealed and complained, steel rubbing against steel along the hub, wood rolling over rutted sun baked earth. The wagon body creaked and groaned as it twisted between smooth ground and rough ridges of baked earth. A multitude of metal pans hung from hooks on the wagon's sides, banging and clanging.

There was no rhythm to the sounds created by the wagon's progress, no sense of harmony. There was only noise, discordant ear-abrasive noise. The wagon rattled ever onward, neither in a rush nor in leisure. Steady it rolled. Steadily and noisily along the rough, rutted road to Pindstein moved the wagon. No dust was stirred by its passing because the Lethbridge road had no dust to stir.

From her second story bedroom window Awbrey's attention had been drawn to the Lethbridge road by a flash of light in the distance. Curious, Awbrey watched the road until she could make out the shape of the wagon drawn by the three brown horses. The low sun hit the pans, the metal reflecting the sunlight with an obscuring glare. Awbrey lingered at the window, watching the wagon silently approach town. Awbrey heard not a sound from that distance. Awbrey shivered.

"That's someone walking over your grave," her grandmother would have said about the shiver.

"Nonsense," her mother would have said. "The grave holds nothing but bones."

The wagon steadily made its way closer to Pindstein, flashing like a faceted gemstone as it swung and swayed, causing the sun to hit its sides at different angles. Awbrey watched it approach, drawn into the image of the lone wagon pulled by its three horses strung out in a line.

The wagon was a vehicle of change. Maybe it heralded change or maybe its coming brought change. Awbrey could imagine the driver, a man of robust character, a competent man. He would need to be competent to strike out into the unknown of the world.

His strong hands would guide horses into the shafts and secure the harnesses with efficiency. If a wheel broke he would have a spare or the tools to make repairs. Whatever came his way as an obstacle to his journey he would be prepared to deal with it.

Awbrey blinked. It was just a wagon. She turned her back to the window and walked to her bed. The Simpsons were coming for dinner. The maid, Jane, had laid out two dresses on Awbrey's bed. Awbrey was to choose between the two dresses. Jane always gave a choice. Awbrey ran her fingertips over the fabric of one of the gowns. The dinner was a special occasion and Jane had laid out two dresses that matched the importance of the evening.

Pindstein was a moderate sized town on the banks of the Maus River in the kingdom of Kiel. The king ruled from Lethbridge, a city evolved from an old fort town high up in the mountains. The Lethbridge road ran through a desolate stretch of land, from the harsh mountain terrain down to rugged foothills and into dry, scrubby flat land. Pindstein was the first town west of Lethbridge but many towns lined the river north and south of Pindstein.

Awbrey was the second child of Hans and Stella Tieg and had passed her seventeenth birthday just over a month ago. The Tiegs were moderately successful. Hans Tieg owned four ships and two warehouses to hold the supplies his ships brought in. Trade was good and provided a decent income. The Tiegs were not the wealthiest family in Pindstein but they were comfortable. Stella Tiegs had started a small boutique when her two children had grown old enough to leave her with time on her hands, which added to the family coffers.

Awbrey had grown up in comfort in a loving family. Her parents could afford to have her educated and she received good marks in school. Awbrey had always been a pleasant looking child with pleasing manners and had grown into a lovely young woman with pleasing manners.

Her nearly black hair matched exactly the shade of her mother's hair, which often prompted comparisons from newly met people. She had round cheeks, full lips, and gently arched eyebrows over brilliant blue eyes. Awbrey's naturally smooth complexion required no face paint or powders to smooth out any flaws.

If Awbrey had any faults it was a tendency to daydream and a need to follow the rules. They were not faults that stood in the way of a young woman who was expecting to marry her childhood love and raise a family. Awbrey had no other goals for her life. To her marrying Eddy Simpson in a year was the best possible future that she could imagine. That night the betrothal would become official even though everyone knew the two would be marrying in a year.

A sound caught Awbrey's attention, pulling her away from the two lovely pink dresses draped across her bed. Awbrey went back to the window and glanced out. The wagon was near the edge of town now, close enough to make out the image of the driver, a man with immensely wide shoulders. He drove with the reins wrapped between his thick fingers, his head covered with a wide-brimmed hat. That was all Awbrey could make out before buildings obscured her view of the wagon.

It was not the wagon that had made the noise that caught her attention. Awbrey was aware of more sounds at the back of her mind but she still watched for the wagon. The road to Lethbridge was traveled often enough that a single wagon was nothing special. Yet Awbrey felt a knot form in her stomach, unable to stop thinking of that wagon and driver.

The noise was Eddy crawling across the porch roof directly under her window. Awbrey gasped when she saw him. Eddy's foot slipped on a tile but he recovered his footing without missing a step. He grinned at her as he scrambled the rest of the way. Awbrey opened the window and leaned out over the sill.

"Are you mad?" Awbrey hissed. "If you break your neck in such stupidity I shall not send flowers to your funeral."

Eddy grinned and vaulted through the open window into her bedroom. "You know that I am half billy goat," he said in greeting.

"That's the problem," Awbrey said. "You are a goat."

Eddy laughed and kissed her cheek. "I wanted to see you. Alone."

"And how are you going to get out again without anyone seeing you?" Awbrey leaned out the window, looking down at the shining, slippery orange clay tiles lining the roof below.

"Same way," Eddy said. His attention was on the dresses on the bed. Both dresses were pink, one a pale pink and one a deeper pink. The pale pink had tulle draped around the skirt. The darker pink had pearls and tiny satin roses sewed along the bodice. Eddy tapped the darker pink dress. "This one." Eddy turned back to Awbrey. "I wanted to tell you the news before dinner. I am going to apprentice for Jacksol in Oakport for a year."

Conflicting emotions swept over Awbrey. She was so proud of him to gain such a wonderful apprenticeship but Oakport was not Pindstein. "Oakport? How wonderful for you. Jacksol is the best in the whole country. But Oakport?"

"It isn't so far," Eddy said. "I can visit every month. When I complete I shall be able to work for him and in a few years buy into the business."

"Oakport?" Awbrey whispered.

"The best news is that he said as long as I do well we can marry after the year of apprenticeship."

"He gave permission?" Awbrey asked, confused. "Why do you need his permission?"

"I will be his apprentice," Eddy said, as if that should explain it all. "We shall have to live in Oakport when we are married. I know that you had your heart set on that house across the street there. Maybe in five years we can manage that."

Voices could be heard in the hall, coming closer. Eddy hurried to the window, pausing only long enough to kiss Awbrey's forehead. With one long, lean leg dangling out the window he grinned and winked at her before stepping out onto the roof. Awbrey watched him run across the clay tiles with her heart in her throat. He really was part goat and made it look simple and easy as he ran to the edge and twisted his body to drop over the edge. Eddy was too confident. Awbrey felt her heart pounding when he vaulted over the roof edge and out of sight.

The bedroom door opened. "Awbrey! Whyever are you not dressed yet?" her mother asked, surprised to see Awbrewy standing at the window still in her cotton day dress.

"Oh," Awbrey said, unable to think of a valid response. She picked up the dress Eddy had chosen. "This one, Jane."

Stella Tieg was a more mature version of her daughter. Their resemblance was almost unnaturally strong. A few gray hairs could be found in Stella's black hair and a few lines had made their mark between her eyebrows but otherwise she showed little signs of age. Her figure was a bit more matronly than her daughter's slim, willowy form. The two would never be mistaken for each other but the resemblance was startling.

Jane had been the Tieg's maid Awbrey's entire life. The elderly woman was stick thin, with a long chin and rheumy blue eyes. Always patient, considerate, and loving, Jane was more like Awbrey's grandmother than a mere maid. The woman appeared to be approaching a hundred years in age yet went about her tasks with the same efficient diligence as if she was only thirty years of age. Stella and Jane were as best of friends as a maid and employer could be.

Jane picked up the other dress and returned it to the wardrobe without a word. Stella stepped up to the window and looked out before sliding the curtains closed. Awbrey slipped out of her day dress, letting it puddle at her feet. Stella took the evening gown and dropped the chosen dress over Awbrey's head. Stella turned Awbrey so that she could do up the laces in the back.

"We have another guest," Stella said, combing out Awbrey's hair. Stella twisted the mass of nearly black hair into a coil and used a comb and clips to hold it in place at the back of Awbrey's head.

"Another guest?" Awbrey asked in alarm. "But we were to discuss me and Eddy tonight!"

"Eddy and me, my dear," Stella said.

"Isn't it Eddy and I?" Jane asked, holding out a tray of jewelry for Stella's selection.

"Oh, who cares?" Awbrey asked in exasperation. She tried turning to face her mother but Stella pushed her shoulder to keep Awbrey's back facing her.

"The pearls," Stella muttered.

"I agree," Jane said, holding up a strand of perfectly round pearls.

"What a horrible day," Awbrey said in a petulant tone as her mother placed jewelry around her neck and in her hair.

"Do not be so dramatic," Stella said.

"Well you won't discuss the marriage with another guest here, will you? First that wagon and then, uh, well it's a lousy day," Awbrey said.

"Yes, well I hardly think one more day will be the end of the world," Stella said. She turned Awbrey and studied the girl. Stella smiled. "You'll do."

"Beautiful," Jane said.

"But tonight was supposed to be the betrothal night," Awbrey said. She meant to give Jane a smile for calling her beautiful but all she could think about was that all her plans were going awry. First

Eddy told her about going to Oakport for a year and now a delay in the official betrothal. It felt like everything was falling apart.

"It wouldn't be proper to not be at the door when our guests arrive," Stella said. "You are ready. Come."

Awbrey sighed. "Fine."

She walked with Awbrey down the hall to the staircase while Jane took the jewelry tray back to the master bedroom. "You have not even asked about our surprise guest," Stella reminded Awbrey.

"I'm sorry. I was just so looking forward to tonight and now it has to wait and Eddy, well, the wagon, well, it's just all upside down now."

"That's the second time you've mentioned a wagon," her mother said. "What wagon?"

"I saw a wagon coming down the Lethbridge road," Awbrey said.

"What a coincidence. Our additional guest just came from Lethbridge."

The Simpsons arrived with their son Eddy and two daughters, Abigail and Sonata. Abigail was a year younger than Awbrey and Sonata just turned ten years old. The family resemblance was strong. Eddy was a younger version of his father and the girls had their mother's auburn hair and hazel eyes but shared the slightly over-sized nose that clearly came from their father.

Proper greetings were done and everyone settled with a drink at hand, lemonade for the girls, hard cider for Eddy and his mother, fine bourbon for Mr. Simpson. Hans Tieg and Mr. Simpson were deep in discussion over the price of dried beef when their final guest arrived.

Stella Tieg opened the door. A stocky man of middle years with broad shoulders stepped into the foyer. Vibrant blue eyes almost glowed under the shadow created by the brim of his hat. A life spent mostly outside had weathered his skin to the color and texture of worn leather. He sported a bushy moustache but the rest of his face was clean shaven.

The man looked rough, even a little intimidating to Awbrey. He would fit in down at the docks, which were filled with rough men, the type of men her father would not allow her to talk to. He looked like he had spent the night before sleeping in a hedge. Dried bits of grass and small sticks had stuck to his clothes and in the braided leather wrapped around where the crown met the brim of his hat. He smelled of horses and dirt.

He immediately removed his wide-brimmed hat and hung it on the hat rack standing next to the door, revealing short cropped hair that had been black at one time but was now mottled gray. The man smiled at Stella and clasped her hands between his for a moment in greeting. Awbrey left Eddy's side to properly greet their guest, as proper manners dictated. He looked like the wagon driver but that could not be possible. The wagon had only just entered the town when her mother had entered her bedroom. Awbrey stared at the man, caught when she met his eyes with her own.

Strength. Awbrey felt the strength in him. He would save her life more than once. He was going to drag her into danger though. Eddy would be hurt. Not climbing over clay tiles but something to do with white, rushing water. There were others this man would be responsible for besides her. It was like they were a family.

Awbrey blinked and took a deep breath. She felt like she had just returned from a long journey instead of just being caught up in imagination spurred by meeting the man's gaze. Her muscles ached and her ears had a dull ringing in them. The man looked at Awbrey thoughtfully. It was as if he knew that she had experienced something. The whole incident took seconds. Awbrey shivered.

Chapter Two

"Welcome to our home, Romke," Stella said, taking the man's hand. "Come. I shall introduce you."

"My daughter, Awbrey," Stella said, gesturing at Awbrey.

"Pleased to meet you," Awbrey said, giving a small curtsey as proper.

"You greatly resemble your mother," Romke said in greeting. "We have met, Awbrey." He smiled. "Perhaps it is not fair to bring up past knowledge of a person when one of the persons was not yet out of leading strings. But I know your mother so well and it is only life's fortunes that have kept me away all these years so that I missed being nothing more than an infant's memory to you."

"Oh," Awbrey said. "Pleased to meet you again."

Romke smiled slightly. "Indeed."

"Mr. and Mrs. Simpson and their son Eddard Simpson."

The man's gaze lingered on Eddy. "Ah, to be twenty again. So much energy at that tender age. I for one had more enthusiasm than sense at your age."

"Abigail and Sonata Simpson," Stella said.

"Lovely doves," Romke said with a warm smile at the two girls.

Abigail and Sonata both smiled prettily at him.

"Our son, Russell, is away on a task. He is learning his father's business."

"Unfortunate," Romke said. "I was hoping to see the boy grown."

"Greetings, Romke," Hans Tieg said, nodding his head. "What can I get you to drink?"

"An ale or pilsner will do. Something to wash away the road's dust is appealing," Romke said.

"You travel from Lethbridge?" Mr. Simpson asked while Hans fetched Romke something to drink.

"Indeed," Romke said.

"Thought so," Mr. Simpson said, nodding. "Not much dust on that road though. It's the clay you see."

"Indeed," Romke said, patting his sleeve and watching the dust rise. "It's not so much clay at higher elevation."

Mrs. Simpson gave her husband a look then smiled at Romke. "What news from the capitol?"

"Ah, the beer," Romke said, taking the mug from Hans. Romke tilted back the mug and drank with enthusiasm, draining the entire mug as everyone watched in surprise. Romke wiped the foam from his moustache with the back of his hand.

"Dinner is ready," Stella said. She gestured toward the dining hall. "Shall we continue our discussions at the table?"

Romke handed Hans his empty mug then offered Awbrey his

arm so that he could escort her to the table. Awbrey politely if reluctantly accepted his arm, glancing at Eddy as she placed her hand on the visitor's arm. Eddy had come up on her other side to escort her to the table. Eddy shrugged when Romke beat him to it. Instead, Eddy pulled his sisters to each side and followed Romke and Awbrey to the table.

Romke pulled out a chair for Awbrey then plopped onto the chair next to her. Eddy seated his sisters opposite them then walked around the table to sit next to Awbrey. Stella frowned slightly as Mr. and Mrs. Simpson stood for a moment surveying the table and open chairs then separated and each sat on either side of their daughters. Jane quietly collected the name place cards that had been ignored and no longer matched.

"Is there news from Lethbridge?" Mr. Simpson asked, continuing the conversation that had been interrupted. "How fares the king?"

"Ah, yes, our beloved king," Romke said, the slightest edge to his voice. "I am not sure if you are aware that the king has acquired a new advisor." Romke looked around the room to gauge the reactions of his audience. The Simpson girls had their heads together and giggled over their private conversation. Eddy was mouthing words to Awbrey. The adults watched Romke with polite interest, yet Stella's attention was clearly on Jane serving the soup. Awbrey elbowed Eddy and jerked her head in Romke's direction.

"Is there something special about this new advisor?" Mrs.

Simpson asked, leaning back as far as she could as Jane ladled soup into her bowl.

"Indeed," Romke said, taking the bread basket and tearing off a large chunk of black bread. "He is against magic. Any magical talent at all."

Mr. Simpson raised one eyebrow. "Magic?"

"Yes, magic. He is convinced that anyone practicing magic is evil," Romke said.

"Magic," Mr. Simpson muttered. "I have heard stories, of course, but magical folk are as rare as two-headed calves. That is absurd. I am more concerned with material matters. Solid matters concern me. There are rumors that there is unrest with the Garlans."

"I have also heard rumors about Garlan," Hans said.

"Indeed," Romke said, staring thoughtfully at Mr. Simpson. "King Olind has a daughter who is reputed to be, uh, of a magical nature. Olind brought the princess along on a visit to Lethbridge a few months ago."

"Did King Eldrid's new advisor insult Princess Sophie?" Eddy asked, attention now engaged.

Romke slurped three spoonfuls of soup before answering. "Indeed. You are sharp, young man."

Awbrey had also immediately considered the connection between a rumored magical princess and sudden aversion to magic but had politely been waiting to hear Romke continue his story instead of blurting out her thoughts. A sense of dread was settling into the pit of her stomach. What kind of advisor was this to insult a princess of a neighboring land just because she might have a magical talent?

If there was a war with Garlan, Eddy could be drafted to fight in that war. There was a standing army but a war would require more soldiers and historically the king drafted men for war. Eddy was not a soldier. Awbrey shifted in her seat. Eddy might even volunteer to join the army without waiting to be drafted. She did not want Eddy to go off to war. They were to be married in a year.

Magic was a faraway thought. People talked about the magical fairy folk in the northern forests but it was just talk. It was common to call a successful merchant a magician but it was said lightly, just a saying. If a wolf appeared friendly to people someone might say the wolf must be a shape shifter and nothing more was thought of it. Awbrey could not understand how anyone thought magic was evil. Magic was just magic and if it existed at all it was like a rainy day was rainy and a summer day could be breezy. How could one hate a rainy day and consider it evil?

Magic did not concern Awbrey. It was someone else's problem. Magic did not affect her. What concerned Awbrey was if a visiting princess was rumored to be magic and some unknown advisor to the king did not like magic and insulted or harmed the Garlan princess. Garlan would surely go to war for such an action. Awbrey did not want Eddy going to war. Her Eddy was not soldier material.

"What is this man's name?" Hans asked.

"Baron Barnett," Romke said. Hans frowned, exchanging glances with Stella. "Yes, I thought you would recognize the name," Romke said, noting the exchange. "Baron Barnett has become the king's new best friend."

"You know the man?" Mr. Simpson asked Hans in surprise.

"Long ago," Hans said.

"Is everyone ready for the next course?" Stella asked, rising to help Jane clear the soup bowls.

Awbrey looked at her mother in surprise. Whoever this Baron Barnett was, hearing his name made her mother nervous. Awbrey glanced at her father. Hans stared into his soup bowl, frowning at his private thoughts. Jane pulled the bowl out from under his gaze and he did not even blink.

"You know the king's advisor?" Awbrey asked. To her it was exciting that her parents could be childhood friends of a powerful baron. Yet they looked so stressed at hearing the news that it made her afraid as well. Neither answered her as Romke was continuing his story.

"As you thought, Baron Barnett was rude to Princess Sophie. More than rude, you might say. There were some minor incidents, er, accidents to the girl while she was at Lethbridge. Nothing could be pinned on the Baron so Eldrid defended his friend and advisor," Romke said. He paused to lovingly savor the aroma drifting up from the plate of food Jane set in front of him. "Ah, rosemary tubers. Delightful."

Awbrey shared Romke's appreciation of the seasoned root and was tempted to follow his lead and dig right in but she patiently waited for everyone to be served as was proper. Awbrey kept a watchful eye on Jane's progress around the table. She held her fork in her hand, poised to stab a tuber the moment the last dish was placed.

"A princess and a magician," Abigail said. She sighed. "How romantic."

"She would be a sorceress, not a magician," her sister, Sonata said.

"Can she turn a pony into a unicorn?" Abigail asked, face lighting up in excitement at the idea.

"Only if she's a virgin," Eddy said lightly without thinking. His cheeks turned red at his mother's steely glare. "Not that she wouldn't be. Being a princess and all. A virgin." The girls giggled when he said that word again.

"I never heard of a magical princess before. What is her magical talent?" Awbrey asked, rushing to Eddy's defense by pulling the attention from him.

"Animals love her," Romke said around a mouthful of hot food.

The Simpson girls were clearly disappointed at such a mundane talent. Then Abigail's face brightened as an idea occurred to her. "You mean she talks to animals?"

"Not that I can say, child. She loves animals and they love her," Romke said, gaze on his plate. "There is no evidence that she actually talks to animals. Just rumors."

Jane brought in the next course on a large tray and set the tray on the serving chest behind the table. Jane removed the empty tuber plates and set down the new plate filled with braised and stuffed game hens at the same time. Awbrey quickly scooped her rosemary tubers onto the plate holding the game hen, earning a scowl from her mother. Awbrey felt no guilt for lack of manners at the table. It was her mother rushing the meal that had forced her to combine the two courses onto one plate. Awbrey was not going to miss out on her rosemary tubers just because her mother decided to rush the dinner.

"We have wonderful news to announce," Mrs. Simpson said, stabbing her last tuber as Jane grabbed her plate and set a new plate with a hen in front of her. "Eddy, please share your news."

All eyes turned to Eddy. He grinned. "I get to apprentice with Jacksol."

"Good for you!" Stella said in delight.

Hans looked up from his plate. "That is marvelous news, boy. The man is very selective."

"Congratulations, Eddy," Awbrey said with a practiced smile. Her lips stuck on her teeth and she smiled broader to free her lip. Her mother frowned at her.

"And there's more," Sonata said, almost bouncing in her chair with excitement.

"The rest must wait," Mrs. Simpson said, putting her hand on the girl's arm.

"Jacksol? Of Oakport?" Romke asked. "What a great honor. Has he said which province you will be groomed for?"

Eddy shook his head. "Nothing definite."

Awbrey frowned. She had not realized that Eddy could be sent to any province in the country. The idea of possibly moving to Oakport already upset her. The thought of moving even farther away, to some city she did not know really upset her. At least she had visited Oakport before, twice as a child.

Awbrey studied Eddy thoughtfully. Looking at him always filled her chest with the greatest loving warmth. Eddy was an average looking young man with a nose a little too big for his face but he had a strong jaw and kind eyes. He was not short nor was he tall. To Awbrey he was just right. He was a kind, thoughtful, and outgoing boy growing into a fine young man. When Awbrey was around Eddy she did not worry about anything. Eddy was both comfortable and wonderful. Eddy might look average to the rest of the world but to Awbrey he was the most beautiful man in the world. She felt like they were two pieces making something whole. Awbrey still did not want to live too far away from her home though.

"You wouldn't stay in Oakport?" Awbrey asked.

"It's a year away, Awbrey. Don't fret," Eddy said softly.

"Oakport? Jacksol would have to retire for Eddy to take over Oakport," Hans said.

"Let's just get through this year," Eddy said. "More concrete options can be addressed then."

Romke nodded thoughtfully. "That is a good approach, son. Sound logic."

The conversation drifted to more neutral topics for a few minutes. Even Sonata had managed to clean her bones before Jane collected that course's plates. Jane returned with flat bowls of fruit, colorful melons cut into bite sized pieces with grapes and strawberries, drizzled with honey and lime juice.

"What is it you do for a living, Mr. Romke?" Mrs. Simpson asked.

"Retired. And it's just Romke. No Mister," Romke said. He chuckled. "I am past the age of great adventures."

Mrs. Simpson frowned. "You are retired from adventuring? That is what you did for a living?"

Romke chuckled again. "Aye. Pretty much. Indeed." He laughed at a private thought.

"I never heard of adventuring for a living," Mrs. Simpson said.

"That's not surprising," Romke said.

There was a dull silence for several minutes. Mrs. Simpson opened her mouth then closed it, shaking her head. Mr. Simpson tried stealing some strawberries from Sonata's plate and the girl put her arm on the table to protect her food from theft. Mrs. Simpson's attention was diverted as she scolded the girl for having her arm on the table.

"I had a dream last night," Abigail said to Awbrey. "I was in a field of flowers and the sun was shining. I could smell the flowers and it was perfect. The field was filled with bees. They hummed as they went from flower to flower. Sometimes they brushed against my hands and arms, all soft and furry and it tickled."

Awbrey smiled. "That is a nice dream. Lots of happy, working bees means that you will be fortunate."

"There's more," Abigail said. "There was a shadow and I looked up. There was a giant baby. Tall enough to block the sun. He had a runny nose and was crying and slapping the bees."

"Marjory said it means she'll marry some poor farmer and have hordes of babies," Sonata said quickly.

"I don't even know any farmer boys," Abigail said, glaring at her younger sister.

"I will have to think about that," Awbrey said. She just did not want to tell Abigail that it meant that someone of a childish nature would cast a shadow on her happiness, maybe even disrupt her life of comfort. If Abigail was a magic user Awbrey would have thought that Romke's news meant that the baby was this Baron Barnett trampling over Abigail's sunny day but that was absurd since Abigail was not a magician. Odd, since Awbrey almost always knew what the dreams meant yet this one did not make sense.

"You interpret dreams?" Romke asked Awbrey.

"Everyone does," Sonata said. "It's just that Awbrey is always right."

"It is Abigail's dream. It's just a matter of understanding the symbols. If I am often right it is just that I know Abigail so well,"

Awbrey said.

"What if someone said reading dreams is magic?" Romke asked. Romke raised his right hand when Stella opened her mouth. It was the slightest gesture. Stella did not say anything.

Everyone at the table laughed. Except Hans and Stella. Awbrey thought it was the silliest thing she had heard. "Magic? Then talking is magic."

"Talking?" Romke asked.

This time Stella laughed. "No one can say my daughter is magic. Look at her. Look at her. Is that the image of evil?" Stella stood. "Excuse me. I must see what is holding up dessert."

"Perhaps we should forgo dessert," Mrs. Simpson said, staring after Stella's retreating back.

"No!" both Simpson girls protested in unison. "Besides, we still have to share the other news," Sonata added.

"Everyone already knows, Sonata," Abigail said.

"I shall assist Stella," Mrs. Simpson said, standing and walking briskly to the kitchen.

"What brings you to Pindstein, Romke?" Mr. Simpson asked.

"Just a stopover," Romke said.

"I hadn't thought you could end up anywhere in the country," Awbrey said to Eddy in a low voice.

"I told you not to fret," Eddy replied in a low voice as well. "I plan to either settle us in Oakport or come back to Pindstein. A year can change all sorts of things, Awbrey. Maybe Jacksol won't hire me after the apprenticeship and you will fret for nothing. Or in a year we will end up in Oakport, having a great adventure."

"I don't like adventures," Awbrey muttered.

"If we have an adventure it will be only the good kind," Eddy promised.

"Oakport is so far away," Awbrey whispered. "I already miss you."

"Not so far," Eddy said. Under the table he took her hand in his, rubbing her thumb with his thumb.

Stella and Mrs. Simpson returned to the table bearing trays filled with bowls of ice cream. The ice cream was filled with nuts and berries. The ice cream held everyone's attention and silence settled over the table, the only sound was of spoons tapping the porcelain bowls. Ice cream was such a special, rare treat. Jane had obviously made the treat to celebrate the agreement of Simpsons and Tiegs agreeing to allow the marriage of their children.

As Abigail had said, everyone already knew that the betrothal was agreed upon. The formal saying when all parties involved were together was required to make the betrothal complete. They would marry. Whether the formal saying was that night or in a week, the date was set and next June Awbrey would marry Eddy. The Hall had already been reserved for a family event. It would take a year to prepare for such a great event and preparations had already been started.

The dinner party moved into the salon to relax on cushioned

chairs and sofas after the large meal. Awbrey and Eddy sat at the game table with game pieces sitting on the square markings before them. Eddy played with a carved dog, twirling it with his long, lean fingers. The game table was just an excuse to gain some sort of privacy in the crowded room.

"What do you think of Princess Sophie being magic?" Eddy asked.

Awbrey moved the pieces around on the game board. A closer look revealed that instead of being aligned to play a game, the carved figures were positioned in pairs posed for kissing.

"If she was magic, why didn't she magic a stop to the baron's tormenting her?" Awbrey asked.

"Maybe it doesn't work that way," Eddy said.

"It doesn't matter," Awbrey said. "Some princess of another land has nothing to do with me."

"If you were magic you would tell me wouldn't you?" Eddy asked.

Awbrey looked up from positioning a carved figure of a man wearing a robe with a basket over his shoulder to kiss a figure with a sun ray headdress. "Of course. But I'm not magic so it doesn't matter."

"It would be neat to talk to animals," Sonata said from below the table. "If I was magic that's what I would want to do. I wonder what a chicken would say?"

Eddy rolled his eyes. "Brat. You are sneakier than a cat. Get out from under there."

"Magic isn't evil," Sonata said, not moving from her spot under the game table. "Magic is wonderful."

"Girls, it's time to leave," Mrs. Simpson announced.

Sonata crawled out from under the table, pushing her skirt down as she stood. Awbrey looked up from the game pieces she had been playing with. Romke still sat on a cushioned chair, feet resting on a hassock, a mug of beer in his hand, and foam on his moustache. Mr. Simpson was already in the foyer, his hat on his head. Awbrey sighed. The betrothal would not be made formal that night.

Awbrey took Eddy's hand and walked to the foyer to say good nights. She stood waiting with her parents as the Simpsons gathered together in the foyer and prepared to leave. There was the scurry to find the girls' wraps while Stella and Mrs. Simpson discussed the recipe for the ice cream. Mr. Simpson stood patiently waiting.

Eddy kissed Awbrey's cheek and whispered in her ear, "If I had magic it would have to be special vision so that I could see under your clothes."

Awbrey laughed as she slapped his arm, her face turning red at the idea of Eddy seeing her without her clothes. Awbrey blushed an even deeper red when her mother frowned at Eddy as if she had heard what he had said. "Don't say that," Awbrey scolded him.

The Tiegs returned to the salon once the door had been shut on the departing Simpson family. Awbrey hesitated at the door, uncertain whether to go her room or join her parents in entertaining their guest. Curiosity over the stranger was stronger than sitting in her room daydreaming about marrying Eddy but it was close. Daydreaming about her upcoming marriage was Awbrey's favorite pastime.

Romke looked up when the Tiegs filed back into the salon. He had been staring morosely into the depths of his beer mug. Romke turned worried eyes to Stella. "Sorry, dear, for ruining your lovely dinner."

"It wasn't ruined in the least," Stella was quick to say.

"Indeed," Romke said with a sad smile. He turned his attention to Awbrey. "What did you see, girl? When I walked into this house, what did you see?"

Awbrey frowned, glancing at her mother. Stella nodded. It was an odd question. Awbrey shrugged then walked to a cushioned chair across from Romke and sat down with her legs curled under her. Stella sat on the arm of the chair Hans settled into next to Romke.

"You wore a large brimmed hat. Though you spoke of dust there was no sign of dust on your clothes," Awbrey said slowly. "Oh, except when Mr. Simpson said something about clay. Then you hit your arm and there was dust."

"I don't think that's what Romke means, dear," Stella said.

"He asked me what I saw. That is what I saw," Awbrey said. She knew. She knew that he meant her impression when looking into his eyes. How could he know that she had seen anything?

"Go on," Romke prodded.

"Strength and adventure. You will save my life. Eddy will be lost in white waters," Awbrey said. She gasped and covered her mouth with both hands.

"I wondered," Stella said. "I noticed the occasional surprise on her face when meeting new people but she never said a word."

"What about the dreams?" Romke asked. "Is Abigail to be knocked up by some farm boy?"

Awbrey sat frozen, hands still over her mouth. She had the strongest desire to blurt out the dream's meaning. Awbrey was stunned that she had told Romke about the impression she had gotten of him. It was an odd little thing that happened sometimes when she first met people. Or sometimes even when she stared directly into a person's eyes. It felt like she would get sucked inside them as the impressions took over.

"The giant baby represents a person who is behaving childishly. Abigail or her family will suffer a loss at the hands of this person. If Abigail is magic it will be because of that. But Abigail isn't magic," Awbrey said. Awbrey sat up straight. "I don't know how you forced me to say it. But it's just her dream not mine. Her mind is using symbols to tell her something."

"I didn't force you to say anything," Romke said.

"You did! I could feel it. I didn't want to say anything."

"It was me, dear," Stella said. Awbrey stared at her mother. "I needed to know," Stella said softly.

"Know what? How could you do that?" Awbrey asked. That

familiar knot tightened even more in the pit of her stomach.

Hans sighed loud enough that Awbrey and Stella both looked at him. Does Baron know we are here?" Hans asked Romke.

"I am sure he will if he doesn't already," Romke said. He leaned forward in his chair. "He has convinced Eldrid to ban all magic. It is illegal to *be* magic, not just practice magic."

"*Be* magic? Stella asked, frowning. "What is it to *be* magic?"

"Whatever Baron Barnett defines it to be. The law *is* defined. I rushed here the moment I learned. It will be a few days before the notices are printed and copied. When they are ready riders will fan out to distribute them. Once they are posted, anyone found to harbor or aid a person of magic will share their punishment."

"What is the punishment?" Hans asked.

"Death," Romke said.

"He wishes the public to flush them out for him," Hans said. He shook his head and his shoulders slumped. "There will be many innocents killed. Anyone will accuse anyone of being magic on a whim or a grudge."

"Indeed," Romke said.

Awbrey watched and listened, filled with uncertainty. She had never seen her mother so upset before. Fear held her tongue still though she wanted to ask a thousand questions, starting with how her mother could trick her into speaking her thoughts when she had not wanted to tell. Awbrey had never told a soul about getting impressions when looking into someone's eyes. Telling her secret left her feeling exposed. She did not want anyone to know.

"Why the rush?" Stella asked, standing and pacing. "Let the rumors run their course and those of magic will fly away. Why the rush to catch them before they can fly?"

"He doesn't want them to fly," Romke said. He stood. "I have two children in the wagon. I should get back to them before they find a way to get into trouble." Romke took Stella's hand. "She will have to come with me. I will collect her in the morning. Do not linger. Delay brings a high price. Hopefully we will be far enough away when the news is made public."

Stella nodded. Tears ran down her cheeks. "Thank you, Romke. We know our course."

"The boy? Your son? Does he show a talent?" Romke asked.

Stella nodded her head. Hans gave himself a shake and stood. "Russell is two days out yet. He will have to stay with us."

"She? Are you talking about me?" Awbrey asked, slowly comprehending what was being discussed. It was suddenly difficult to breath. "I am not leaving with you. I have school. I don't even know you. I am going to marry Eddy next year."

Chapter Three

"If you stay here they will come for you," Stella said. "They will find you and they will hurt you. If you go with Romke he can get you safely away. To a place where they can't hurt you." Stella knelt beside Awbrey. "Do you understand, Awbrey? With Romke there is a chance to survive this. If you stay there is no doubt that you will be arrested."

"But I've done nothing wrong!" Awbrey wailed. Tears streamed down her cheeks as she looked at her mother. Her beautiful, sweet mother looked up at her with red, swollen eyes.

"That doesn't matter, Awbrey," Stella said, wiping the tears from Awbrey's cheeks.

"It isn't fair," Awbrey complained.

"No, it isn't fair," Hans said. He put his hand on Stella's shoulder and the other hand on Awbrey's hand. "Awbrey, it is time to go up to your room and pack one bag with essentials. Then you will close your eyes and sleep until we wake you in the morning. In the morning you will leave with Romke without a fuss. A great adventure awaits you. In a year you will marry Eddy but until then you will finish your schooling with Romke. Now go to your room."

Awbrey sobbed but nodded her head. It was not fair. She had done nothing wrong. Awbrey looked up at her father. "Can we not stand against them? We should stand against them."

"Not this time, my precious daughter," Hans said, voice cracking. He cleared his throat.

"Hush," Stella said to Awbrey. "Do not talk about standing against the king's law. That is treason."

Awbrey looked from her father to her mother and back again. "What about you? Will they arrest you if I go?"

"That is why you must go before the announcement," Romke said. "If you go before the announcement no one will think anything of it. If the announcement comes and then you fly it will bring attention on you."

"And Eddy will be safe," Awbrey whispered.

She looked up at Romke. It was time to go to her room and when she woke her whole life would be uncertain. Except she would still marry Eddy in a year. As long as she could still marry Eddy in a year then the rest would be bearable. Hopefully in a year things would be straightened out and this business of anyone thinking she was magic would be set aside as the nonsense that it was.

Awbrey stood and left the salon in a daze, not even saying farewell to Romke or good night to her parents, overwhelmed by the news. It could not be real though she knew that it was. Upon reaching her room she realized that she had to fetch a travel bag from the attic. By the time Awbrey had retrieved the travel bag and mindlessly stuffed clothes into the bag she was so tired that her eyes hurt.

A noise woke Awbrey. She lay on the bed, half asleep as she pondered what could have created the noise. It was too much effort to move so she snuggled deeper under the down filled duvet instead of getting up to investigate the noise. Dawn had barely lightened the sky outside her window.

The noise came again, a tap tap at the window. Only Eddy would be at her window. Goosebumps covered her bare arms when she slipped out of the warmth beneath the blankets. Awbrey hurried to the window and pushed aside the drapes. There was Eddy, slipping on the roof tiles as he was walking on the roof, away from the window. He easily corrected his balance and quickly reached the edge, glancing back up at the window before swinging over the roof edge. Just as he dropped over the edge he looked up and saw Awbrey in the window. His face lit up in the meager light but he was already committed to dropping off the roof and vanished from sight.

There was a sharp rap on the bedroom door and Stella entered the room. "It is time, Awbrey."

Awbrey turned. "In a moment. Please."

"There is no time," Stella said. She set the light she carried onto the bureau. "Jane set out a dress last night after you went to bed. Here, sit. I will do your hair. A simple braid, I think."

Awbrey glanced behind her out the window. There was no sign of Eddy on the roof. Beyond the neighboring houses the sky was no longer black but neither had the sun yet risen so a wall of gray covered the horizon. Awbrey pulled the drapes shut and removed her nightgown. Stella handed her articles of clothing and Awbrey dressed without paying attention to what she wore.

"I didn't get a chance to say farewell to Eddy," Awbrey said.

"We shall tell him," Stella said. "Sit. Did you already pack your comb?"

"I should at least write a note," Awbrey said.

Stella did not reply right away. She found a comb and worked on Awbrey's hair for several minutes. Her mother's hands shook as she tried to braid Awbrey's hair. Awbrey was about to ask her mother if she had not slept well when Stella spoke. "I suppose you may tell him that you are traveling south with your uncle. For your last year of schooling."

"Uncle?" Awbrey asked.

"Well, great uncle. He is my uncle. But who says Great Uncle Romke?" Stella said.

"He is my uncle?" Awbrey repeated in surprise. Something else her mother said grabbed her attention. "South?" Awbrey perked up. "Then we go to Oakport?"

"Not to. Possibly through," Stella said. She finished Awbrey's hair and picked up the travel bag, grunting at the weight. "Come, Awbrey."

"But the note."

"You can write it in the salon," Stella said.

Romke had already arrived. He sat at the dining table eating a hearty breakfast. Scrambled eggs, a pile of sausages, and biscuits dripping with honey filled the plate in front of him. A basket covered with a towel sat on the table next to him. A covered plate sat across the table. Awbrey's breakfast.

"Good morning," Awbrey said to Romke as she hurried past him to the salon.

"Good morning," Romke said around a mouthful of steaming food.

Stella used both hands to carry the travel bag to the foyer. Awbrey sat at the small writing desk in the salon and pulled out parchment, ink, and nub. She dipped the nub in the ink and sat with a blank mind, unable to find the words to tell Eddy that she was leaving without saying farewell in person.

Eventually the words came to her, much as her mother had spoken them. When Awbrey finished the note she sanded the ink, folded the parchment at all four corners, and sealed the created flaps with wax. Writing Eddy's name on the outside of the folded note brought tears to her eyes as the pain of leaving her beloved began anew. Awbrey left the note on the desk and walked to the dining table.

"Eat, child," Romke said when Awbrey stared at her breakfast plate.

"I have no appetite," Awbrey said.

"Eat anyway," Romke said. "It may be nightfall before you have a hot meal again."

Awbrey sat across from Romke and ate. Despite her lack of appetite she managed to eat a whole plateful of food, even a second biscuit dripping with honey. For some reason she now felt eager to leave. Romke seemed to take forever to eat his breakfast.

Hans and Stella stood in the foyer waiting when Awbrey and Romke left the dining hall. They hugged their daughter farewell then stepped back. Hans had his arm around Stella, comforting his wife. Romke handed Awbrey the basket to carry and picked up the travel bag. Awbrey did not want to leave yet she felt eager to get out the door.

"What about Russell?" Awbrey asked, feeling horrible that she had not given thought to her brother. "I should write a note to Russell as well."

"We shall explain it to him," Hans said. "May the wind be at your back, warm sunshine on your cheeks, and a song in your heart."

"And no dragons in your beer," Awbrey said automatically to complete the traveler wish.

"And if there be dragons in your beer, try the ale," Romke said.

The joke almost made Awbrey smile. Almost. One corner of her mouth twitched like she was going to smile. It was with a heavy heart that Awbrey left her home so early in the morning that even the birds yet slept. The streets were silent as well. Awbrey did not look back. It was ill luck to look back when starting a journey. Even when she felt an itch in her back, Awbrey did not turn around and look to see if Eddy was hanging out on the roof or look for one last glance at her parents.

The inn Romke had chosen to stay at was only a few minutes' walk away from the Tieg house. Romke's wagon sat in the inn's yard with the three horses harnessed in tandem, ready to go. Romke walked to the side of the wagon and dropped Awbrey's travel bag into a lidded wood box bolted to the wagon wall.

Awbrey stared at the wagon. It was more like a miniature house on wheels. She stood holding the basket handle in both hands, letting the basket dangle at the end of her arms as she stared up at the assortment of pots, pans, saws, shovels, and other tools she did not recognize either lashed in place or hanging from hooks bolted to the sides. They would wake the whole town when they left if they made as much noise as she expected they would once the wagon started moving.

Romke reached down and took the basket from her. "Let's meet my other two passengers, shall we?" he said.

At the rear of the wagon two metal steps hung down from a blue painted door. Romke opened the door and gestured for Awbrey to climb inside ahead of him. Awbrey hesitated, took a deep breath, and stepped up and peered inside. It really was a small house.

Two cushioned benches lined each side, serving as sofas. A small black stove stood opposite the door. A lantern sat on the cold stove, casting a warm glow that touched the entire wagon interior. Awbrey did not notice any more details of the wagon's interior once she set eyes on the two people sitting inside, her attention held on the two occupants.

"Keep going," Romke said.

Awbrey stepped through the door. Romke followed. He handed the basket to a young, frail looking blonde woman. "Breakfast," he said. "Awbrey, this is Sophie. The boy is Jaydin. Get to know each other."

Introductions done, Romke shut the door. Awbrey turned her head to look at Jaydin. Romke had the distinct habit of referring to anyone under forty as boy or girl. Though Jaydin was not forty neither was he a boy. Dark of hair and muscular of limb, he had to at least be in his mid-twenties if not upper twenties. Jaydin nodded at Awbrey in greeting but his attention was on the food Sophie revealed by pushing the towel aside.

"You'll want to sit quickly," Jaydin said just before cramming half a biscuit in his mouth. Scrambled eggs squeezed out the sides of the split biscuit.

The wagon jerked slightly. Awbrey hurried to the other side of Sophie and almost made it to the free space on the sofa when the wagon jerked into motion, sending her backwards onto Sophie's lap instead of on the intended spot on the sofa. Mortified, Awbrey turned and threw herself onto the empty side of the sofa. The sofa was really a wood bench with cushions and it was a rear end bruising landing. Sophie did not respond at all to the fact that Awbrey had just fallen onto her.

"Oh, look, Jayd, honey," Sophie said in delight. Her voice was soft, just as she was frail and cultured.

"Sophie? Like Princess Sophie?" Awbrey asked, staring at Sophie. They were roughly the same age, give or take a year. Sophie looked like a princess, Awbrey thought.

"When Princess Sophie was born half the girls in the kingdom were named Sophie for several years," Sophie said.

Awbrey nodded. It was true. She knew at least five girls in school with the name Sophie. It was just that this Sophie felt like a princess. Awbrey could not have explained why she felt that way. She had never met a princess before but this Sophie was exactly how she imagined a princess would be.

Sophie was elegantly beautiful. Her hair was so blonde it was almost white. She wore it long and loose. It shimmered around her face, a long face with a broad forehead. Awbrey realized that she was staring but could not help herself. There was something about Sophie that held the eye. The girl was so frail looking, like she would float away in a strong breeze. She spoke slowly, in a fuzzy voice and moved languidly, like a wave washing up on a river bank.

"What talent brings you to our growing group?" Jaydin asked. He did not even look up at Awbrey when he asked because his attention was on the contents of the basket.

"Talent? I have no talent," Awbrey said, pulling her gaze from Sophie to look at Jaydin.

Jaydin looked up at Sophie. The frail girl turned her head to study Awbrey. Sophie frowned. "Perhaps you believe that you don't but you must, you see. It is the ticket to enter this journey in Uncle Romke's wagon."

"Uncle Romke? He is your uncle as well?" Awbrey asked in surprise. "We are cousins?"

"Can you read it?" Jaydin asked Sophie.

Sophie shook her head. "It could be something to do with reading. I feel no active talent."

The wagon moved through the town with only occasional clangs. The town's roads were not rutted and the wagon moved at a sedate pace, creating minimal swaying. Eventually the wagon picked up speed, signaling that they had passed beyond the town's boundaries.

"If we tell you ours will you tell us yours?" Jaydin asked Awbrey.

Awbrey stared at him but chose not to reply. Awbrey did not want to talk. Feelings of loss and despair washed over her, growing stronger the farther they moved from Pindstein. Awbrey only wanted to sink into those feelings. The calm that had allowed her to meekly follow Romke out of her house and into this wagon was fading and panic growing in its place.

"I'll go first," Jaydin said. "I am a shape shifter."

A shape shifter. That was just a myth. Everyone knew that shape shifters lived in Darner's hidden forest to the north. They could not cross the sandy desert surrounding the forest. Plus, they had no features, which enabled them to shift into something else. Awbrey wanted to cry. Her chin trembled. She was being taken away from her home and family and placed with these two who seemed to be playing games at her expense.

"I can do two things," Sophie said, looking at Awbrey. "I can communicate with animals. And I can sense other's talent."

"Now your turn," Jaydin said.

Awbrey stared at Jaydin. He had curly black hair and his skin was the color of cooked honey, a deep golden. Even sitting it was clear that he was a tall man. His arms were long and angular more than muscular. His nose was broad and turned up slightly. Jaydin had kind eyes. They were a deep, dark brown and when he looked at her Awbrey felt his sincerity and kindness, so at odds with his having sport with her. Maybe he believed that he was a shape shifter.

"I have no magic," Awbrey said.

"I feel something," Sophie said thoughtfully, more to herself.

"I can understand people's dreams. That is just learning the symbols. Not magic at all. Lots of people can do that. Lots of people do that," Awbrey said.

Sophie continued to study Awbrey, nodding as Awbrey talked. "You can see the future," Sophie said. "It is really hard for me to sense but it is there. But only when it affects you. The dreams must allow you to see other's futures." Sophie sat back on the sofa, turned slightly to face Awbrey. "Oh, Baron Barnett would surely be after you. That's how he convinced Eldrid to pass the ban on magic.

Destiny being changed by readers. Eldrid is big on destiny."

"Stop it," Awbrey said, covering her ears with her hands. "I just learned the dream language. It's just symbols."

Sophie did a head shrug, pursing her lips as she stared at Awbrey. "It's wearing off. Someone put a glamor on you and it's wearing off. That's why you feel so overwhelmed. It will fade. That is better than you just being a spoiled little girl pouting."

"Leave me alone," Awbrey muttered.

Awbrey leaned back on her seat, pulling away from them as far as she could manage in such tight quarters. The rattling wagon was annoying her nerves. As they left the well maintained road near the town the pans hanging from the wagon walls were clattering and banging and the wagon swayed with each bump or rut in the road.

If she had magic she would know it. Awbrey firmly believed that. She would be able to do things. Special things. The wagon moved steadily along the road, swaying and rocking gently, gaining a rhythm now that eventually calmed Awbrey's rattled nerves. The noise of the banging pots and pans receded. Awbrey took a deep breath. She was not magic. Awbrey did not know why her parents had sent her away with Romke because she was not magic.

Jaydin had cleaned out any last crumb from the basket using his fingers. When he was finally satisfied that nothing remained he set the basket aside and leaned back on the sofa. He closed his eyes and immediately fell asleep.

"There is nothing to fear," Sophie said to Awbrey. "He will not turn into a wolf or bear in here, though he may eat like one."

Awbrey had been staring at Jaydin when Sophie spoke and she quickly averted her gaze. It was not polite to stare. "I am not afraid. Shape shifters aren't real."

"Jaydin is very proper. Have you ever seen a bear wearing pants?" Sophie asked. The frail girl giggled.

"I don't understand," Awbrey admitted.

Sophie decided not to pursue the topic. "Uncle Romke told us about you. Oh, not your talent. He told us that we were collecting the Tieg's daughter," Sophie said. "Romke's younger brother was your mother's father. Do you understand what that means?"

"That he is my great uncle?" Awbrey said questionably.

"There is that. What I was pointing to is that Uncle Romke is a lot older than he seems."

"How is he your uncle?" Awbrey asked. There were no degrees of old to a seventeen year old girl. Old was just old.

"He was married to my grandfather's sister," Sophie said. Awbrey's gaze moved to the sleeping Jaydin. A soft snore came from the man and his mouth hung open. Sophie followed Awbrey's gaze. The blonde girl smiled fondly at Jaydin. "Romke's father was married to a woman who had a child from another marriage and that girl was Jaydin's grandmother."

Awbrey tried to absorb the information. It was almost overwhelming to discover an expanded family. The information thrown at her when she had no idea of their existence took time to absorb. It did help direct her thoughts from her situation as she tried to piece together what Sophie was saying.

"How do you know all that?" Awbrey asked.

"How do you not?" Sophie asked.

"I never even heard of Romke before last night," Awbrey said. "My parents never talked about any family outside of us. My grandparents are all gone. It's just us. Or at least I thought it was just us."

The window above the sofa Jaydin slept on gradually made its presence known as the sky lightened. Awbrey stared up at the narrow strip of glass. She had not even realized that there was a window. There was a matching window above the sofa Sophie and she sat upon. The window was only a few inches below the roof and stretched lengthwise over two feet but was only about six inches high.

As more and more light flooded into the wagon there was no longer a need for the lantern. Sophie turned the knob on the lantern and the flame inside fluttered then went out. The acrid smell of the brief bit of smoke from the wick tickled Awbrey's nose and she sneezed several times. The blonde girl opened a bag near her feet and pulled out an embroidery hoop with fabric stretched inside the wood circles. Sophie moved around on her seat until the sun fell directly on the hoop then concentrated on stitching.

Awbrey leaned her cheek against the back of the sofa cushion and watched the embroidery hoop without really seeing it. Sophie's long, fragile fingers held a needle with green thread, pushing it into the fabric then pulling it out, thread making a squeaking sound as it passed through the fabric. The swaying wagon made Awbrey sleepy. Sophie's embroidery movements fell into a rhythm with the swaying wagon. Awbrey's eyes grew heavy.

Nothing felt real. It was like a haze covered her brain. Last night Awbrey was expecting her betrothal to Eddy be made official and instead that morning she was riding away from home in a wagon with distant cousins so many times removed that she had never heard of them before, to a place unknown. Awbrey's stomach tightened in knots and she jerked fully awake. The wagon rumbled along the road to the unknown.

Eventually Awbrey's tiredness overtook her mind's fretting and she fell asleep sitting with her cheek on the cushion forming the back of the sofa. Awbrey woke when the wagon stopped moving. She wiped the drool from her chin and winced at the stiffness in her neck from sleeping in such an awkward position. She was still sitting up, leaning sideways against the back of the sofa. Sophie was already standing at the door with her head down, back bent, waiting for Romke to open the door. Jaydin sat on his sofa, stretching his arms and shoulders.

The wagon started moving again and Sophie's shoulders slumped in disappointment but she remained standing where she was, head down to keep it from hitting the ceiling. Jaydin craned his neck to look out the high set window above Awbrey's head. Awbrey looked up at the window above Jaydin's head. Only blue sky was visible. Awbrey stood and stepped onto the sofa, intending to look out the window above her.

"Wait," Jaydin said. Awbrey froze. "We don't know what's out there. No faces in the window."

Awbrey frowned. She glanced back at Jaydin thoughtfully. No one had said rules about looking out windows. That being Romke. Awbrey stretched up to peer out the window. There was nothing worth seeing. There were trees in the distance and a cultivated field between the wagon and the trees. Awbrey dropped back down and stepped off the sofa.

"Why did you do that?" Jaydin asked in surprise.

"I wanted to see," Awbrey said. "There is nothing to see anyway."

"You shouldn't do that," Jaydin said, shaking his head. "What's the point of hiding in this wagon if you just go sticking your face in the window for all to see?"

The wagon made a sharp right hand turn, sending Sophie sliding along the back wall. The girl pulled herself up and resumed her post at the door.

Awbrey nearly jumped out of her skin when a section of the front wall opened and Romke stuck his head through the opening. "It won't be but a few minutes yet, Sophie."

Sophie nodded but did not turn, her face pressed up against the door. Romke pulled his head back and the wall shut with a swish.

Awbrey looked at Sophie in concern, not sure what was happening. Awbrey opened her mouth to ask what was happening, how Romke had known that Sophie wanted out, how had Sophie known that Romke planned to stop but she kept her questions to herself.

Awbrey looked up where Romke's head had appeared. Her cheeks burned in embarrassment even though she had not asked the foolish questions out loud that had been running through her head. It was a shutter that slid open. Awbrey could see the small crack where the two doors met and the frame around the opening in the wall between the driver's seat and the interior of the wagon where the doors slid out of sight when the shutters were opened.

Sophie was now doing the leg dance in place. The girl crossed her ankles and bounced up and down impatiently. She simply needed to relieve her bladder and obviously had let Romke know through the opening. Awbrey felt like a silly child, spooked by something as simple as a nature break.

All this magic talk had her jumping at shadows. Awbrey's head felt less hazy after her nap. It was like she had been walking in a fog since her father told her to go pack a bag and prepare to leave with Romke in the morning. Awbrey had even gone immediately to sleep until woken as instructed.

Awbrey frowned. If she was to be with Romke for a year she could not marry Eddy in a year. It would take a year to prepare for the wedding. It had felt logical hearing her father say it the night before but now there was no logic to it at all. Awbrey wished she had resisted. She should have done something besides meekly walk away with Romke.

The wagon lurched to a stop and less than a minute later the back door opened. Sophie flew down the steps and walked stiffly but quickly out of sight. Jaydin stood and walked to the door bent over because he was too tall to stand completely upright inside the wagon. He bounded out behind Sophie. Awbrey stretched and casually followed, exiting the wagon cautiously. They were in a tree-lined meadow.

"Pick your tree, girl," Romke said, waving his arm towards the trees at the meadow's edge. "Stretch your legs a bit. We will eat a bite then be on the road again."

Awbrey waited for Jaydin to walk back into sight before picking a direction and weaving between the trees until she felt securely out of view from anyone. When she returned to the meadow Romke gestured for her to join him. He had filled three buckets with water from a barrel on the side of the wagon. He picked up two buckets and told her to bring the last bucket.

Awbrey frowned. Jaydin joined them and took one of the buckets from Romke. The two men walked to the horses and held them for the horses to drink. Awbrey stared at the bucket in surprise. He expected her to water the horse like she was a groom. It was not that she was against doing the chore, she was just momentarily stunned into inaction.

Grudgingly Awbrey picked up the bucket and lugged it to the

last horse. The horse whinnied deep in its chest before plunging its head into the bucket and drinking deeply. Awbrey had to brace the bucket against her stomach to keep it up high enough for the horse to drink. The horse kept pushing down on the bucket as it drank.

Sophie came up behind her. "His name is Black Star," the frail girl said to Awbrey. Sophie twirled the horse's forelock out of his eyes as he drank. The horse raised his head and snorted, blowing water all over Awbrey. Sophie laughed even though she had gotten her share of spray. "This one here is Fall Moon. The one up front is Running Water."

"They are Jack, Brownie, and Bean," Romke said, walking back to them. He took the bucket from Awbrey and kept walking.

"That's just what Romke calls them," Sophie said. She gave Black Star a final pat and followed Romke.

Awbrey looked at the horse. Big brown eyes stared back at her. Awbrey tentatively gave the horse a pat on the neck before joining the rest of the group at the back of the wagon. Romke was rummaging through a barrel lashed to the rear side of the wagon. Awbrey smelled her hand and wrinkled her nose. She now smelled like horse.

"It will be a cold lunch," Romke said. "Why are you huddling around me? Stretch your legs. Here, hold this first," he said, holding out a paper wrapped package to Awbrey.

Sophie hurried around the side of the wagon and out of sight. Awbrey patiently held the packages and canvas bags that Romke placed in her arms as he peered and sorted through the barrel. He finally found what he was looking for and started putting away the items Awbrey held for him, occasionally looking inside a package before deciding whether it stayed out or went back into the barrel.

"How long will it take to get where we are going?" Awbrey asked.

"Oh, awhile yet," Romke said.

"I did not bring any books. Do you have books?" Awbrey asked.

"Books?" Romke asked, looking up from a bag of cornmeal.

"I have nothing to do. I may as well study while cooped up in the wagon," Awbrey said.

"Indeed. Aye, books. I have some books under one of the benches," Romke said. He shoved the bag of cornmeal into the barrel and shut the lid. "Help yourself."

They ate their lunch standing. Romke pared a slice of hard cheese from a cheese wheel for each of them, broke a round loaf of dark brown bread into quarters, one for each, and passed out apples. Romke looked up at Jaydin thoughtfully. He cut two more slices of cheese and gave them to the young man before packing the cheese back into the barrel. They drank water from the water barrel with a ladle tied to the barrel. Romke passed around a jar of pickled peppers, which Awbrey passed on to Jaydin without taking one herself.

Romke was impatient to get on the road again so the lunch break was brief. The second they had all finished eating he ushered them back into the wagon and shut the door.

While the wagon lurched and swayed over rough ground with Romke guiding it back to the road Jaydin helped Awbrey search for books under the sofa. They both crouched in front of the sofas while Sophie stood next to them, holding tightly to keep from falling. They lifted the cushions of first one then the other sofa. Awbrey got on her hands and knees to look for a cubby or door but had no luck finding one. Jaydin ran his hands along the top of the wood base and pressed here and there with no result.

"He said under one of the benches. It must open," Awbrey said in frustration.

"If he has books it is probably on mining or building tools," Sophie said, watching them.

"Uncle Romke was a miner?" Awbrey asked in surprise, looking up at Sophie.

"No. It was just the most boring subject I could think of," Sophie said.

The blonde girl leaned over Awbrey, staring at the bench top. The bench had a lip around it to hold the cushions in place. Awbrey was almost on her face beneath Sophie. Because Sophie was crowding her space Awbrey saw the small glint of metal flush with the bottom lip.

Awbrey was eye level with the metal. She crouched even lower to get a different perspective. "It's a hinge," she said. Jaydin leaned over her to get a better look at what she saw. Awbrey had elbows and knees pressing her down even further.

Sophie looked down at Awbrey. "Oh, sorry," she said, immediately backing off Awbrey's hair.

"Got it," Jaydin said. He was still blocking Awbrey from getting up from the floor though his knee was not in her side any longer.

When Jaydin opened the bench light peeked through a gap in the corner. Another hinge was visible but this one was vertical. Awbrey pushed against Jaydin so that she could stand. Jaydin sat back to allow Awbrey to get up off the wagon floor. Jaydin studied the contents under the bench, head tilted as he looked. Awbrey peered into the storage space.

"No books here," Jaydin said. Sophie immediately went to the other bench when she saw the piles of blankets, old clothes, and metal tools inside the bench they had been struggling to open. "Books here," Sophie called.

Awbrey still looked inside the bench she knelt next to. It was not as long inside as outside. She pushed the blankets out of the way and pushed her hand along the side. There was a small latch. Awbrey thoughtfully traced the contours of the latch with her fingertips.

"No," Jaydin said, putting his hand on hers.

"But there's a hidden compartment," Awbrey said.

"Which is not meant for us to invade," Jaydin said.

Chapter Four

Awbrey looked up at Jaydin. He was right. She had gotten so caught up in the hunt that she had stopped thinking about anything but finding hidden treasure. Romke had a hidden compartment for privacy. Awbrey stared at the inside of the bench, the urge to see what was hidden was almost overwhelming but she resisted. Awbrey pushed the blankets back in place over the hidden compartment and shut the lid over the bench.

Sophie had already pulled out several books that did not interest her. She knelt in front of the right bench and pulled out a book, made a face when she read the title, and set the book on a growing pile of books next to her. Awbrey scooted over to the other bench and picked up the top book on the discarded pile.

The book was bound in leather with gold inlaid lettering on the spine and on the cover. Instead of reading the title, Awbrey opened it and looked for a table of contents. The distinct odor of old book filled her nostrils as she turned the pages. The paper was old and yellowed with water stains on the top right edge of many of the first pages.

The book was divided into two parts, *The Rise of Kiel* and *The*

Fall of Kiel. The book's title was simply *Kiel History: The Tiegens*. Awbrey titled her head as she stared at the table of contents. She flipped the book to look at the title on the spine then flipped it back to look at the contents page again. Awbrey had never heard of the Tiegens and the similarity to her surname interested her.

Awbrey turned to the first page and started reading. She had heard the name King Frednil but had never known any details about him. His reign had been hundreds of years ago and his name was just a relic of the past listed as reference for modern kings. The rise of Kiel began with King Frednil, a great and just leader.

Sophie had finished pulling out all the books and found nothing of interest in the titles on the spines. "Nothing on mining but just as boring," she said.

Awbrey looked up from her reading. She clutched *The Kiel History: The Tiegens* against her chest and picked up another book from Sophie's discarded pile. *Garlan History: The Tiegens*. Awbrey held onto that one without even opening it. Awbrey tilted her head and read the titles of the stacked pile of books. They all looked so interesting that she wanted to read them all.

"I will start with these two," Awbrey said. "If you don't want to read any we should put the rest away for now. Can you show me how you opened the bench?"

Sophie smiled and put the books away so that she could shut the bench and then open it for Awbrey to see how it was done. Awbrey watched then opened the bench to make sure that she understood.

The bench popped right open once she knew the right place to push. There was a small hole in the lip and pushing it made the bench cover pop right up.

Once they replaced the cushions Sophie settled on a spot in the sun with her embroidery. Awbrey sat next to her and opened the Kiel history book with the Garlan history book on her lap. Jaydin stretched out on his sofa and closed his eyes. The wagon rumbled and swayed, steadily putting Pindstein further and further away.

The history book held Awbrey's interest for several hours but even reading about how King Frednil led Kiel into prosperity until he fell in love with the married queen of Iberland and risked his entire kingdom's fate could not suppress the discomfort of sitting for hours. Awbrey set the book down and stretched. She laced her fingers together and raised her hands above her head, twisting and stretching then moved her laced hands behind her head and twisted twice more.

"Did you come from Lethbridge then?" Awbrey asked Sophie as she dropped her hands and relaxed against the sofa cushion.

Sophie set down her embroidery hoop and looked across to Jaydin, who had opened his eyes when Awbrey spoke. "We were both in Lethbridge when Uncle Romke grabbed us and rushed to Pindstein, yes." Sophie said.

"So this is your second day in this wagon? How can you stand it?" Awbrey asked.

"It is better than being in Eldrid's prison," Jaydin said. He still lay on his back with his legs hanging over the end of the sofa.

"Why would King Eldrid make being magic a reason to arrest someone? I could see if someone used magic to break a law. But just being magic is, well, silly."

"Silly?" Sophie asked. The blonde girl looked offended at the word. "You think being magic is silly?"

"Making magic illegal is silly," Awbrey said, going on the defensive. "I've never even known anyone magic. If there are magic people they are obviously not going around causing trouble. How can he just suddenly announce it's illegal to be who you are?"

"Oh. If you have ever met Baron Barnett it would make more sense," Sophie said. She shivered when she said the man's name.

"Meeting him would not change that," Awbrey said, shaking her head.

"He considers himself a pious man. He thrives on telling people that he is a pious man. He believes that everyone has a destiny. All the future is laid out in a grand plan. He has decided that people of magic are capable of disrupting the grand plan. Disrupting the grand plan will bring about chaos," Sophie explained.

Awbrey's mouth dropped open. "You are serious. How can King Eldrid listen to such madness?"

"Because King Eldrid believes Baron Barnett," Jaydin said. He sat upright. "Baron Barnett has convinced the king that destiny has great plans for him but someone of magic could ruin everything. So everyone of magic must be destroyed."

"If it is destiny how can it be stopped? Isn't destroying those born magic disrupting destiny?" Awbrey asked, puzzled. "Wait. Destroyed?"

"It is now a death sentence to be magic," Sophie said softly. "You may think it's "silly" but people will die because of this new law."

Awbrey shivered. She looked from Sophie to Jaydin and back again. They were serious. Awbrey looked down at the book in her hand without really seeing it. Her parents had not sent her away for a year. They had sent her away forever. Eddy. Awbrey would never marry Eddy, maybe never even see him again. It was so unfair. She had never done anything wrong. She was not even magic.

Awbrey looked up at Sophie. Why would anyone want to kill the frail, blonde girl who gave horses fancy names? Awbrey looked at Jaydin. Why would anyone want to kill the quiet, hungry, sleepy young man? It was not right. The wrongness made her want to stand on top of a mountain and scream out her frustration to the whole world.

The sun was close to the horizon but it was still light out when Romke opened the shutters and yelled back that he was going to visit a farmhouse ahead. He planned to ask their permission to camp on their land and maybe buy a chicken or two for their dinner. They were to stay inside the wagon and be as quiet as mice.

The farmer agreed to both of Romke's requests and they made camp about a mile from the farm yard in a copse of trees with two chickens to roast. The spot was quite similar to where they had stopped for the midday meal, a grassy area surrounded by trees, just more cozy. Jaydin helped Romke unharness the horses and tie them to stakes so they could graze. Romke had chosen the spot because a clear stream ran through the trees. The trees also provided some privacy from the road.

Awbrey sat on the ground with her back against a wagon wheel, absorbed in the enormity of what she had learned. Sophie wandered along the edge of the trees collecting fallen branches for the fire. Awbrey could hear the horse's crunching the grass as they grazed. A bird twittered in a tree nearby. A rabbit hopped into view, raising its head to study the area, its nose twitching. A bee buzzed by her head, lingering for a moment before moving on to find pollen in the flowers dotting the tall grass.

"Well water," Romke said, setting a bucket with a ladle next to Awbrey. "Only for drinking and cooking. Wash with stream water."

Awbrey stared at him but made no response. Romke grunted and stared at her thoughtfully for a few minutes before going back to his tasks. In a short time the two chickens were skewered on a long branch resting on two forked branches he had stuck into the ground on either side of the fire. Jaydin was set to watch the roasting birds and turn the stick periodically. Romke had purchased eggs and milk as well and mixed up some cornbread in a pan which he put on a brick at the edge of the fire.

"Did you drink, girl?" Romke asked coming up to her. Awbrey

looked at the bucket but did not reply. Romke filled the ladle and put it in her hand. "Drink."

Awbrey put the ladle to her mouth and took a swallow. The water was wonderful, clean and tasteless on her tongue. She drank the entire ladleful then filled the ladle and drained it again. Romke nodded in satisfaction.

"Now tell me what ill humor has you in its grip," Romke said, kneeling beside her.

Just thinking about it brought tears to Awbrey's eyes and she could not speak if she had wanted to. She would never marry Eddy because the king would have her killed even though she had done nothing wrong. It was a lot to process and too painful to discuss.

"Reality has just set in, eh?" Romke said. "Good. Then you will realize how serious this is. My goal is to keep you out of the hands of those who seek to do you harm. If you help me it will make my job easier."

Romke was right. He was taking her to a place where the king could not harm her. Or Sophie. Or Jaydin. This wonderful man was saving her life. Awbrey threw herself at Romke, wrapping her arms around him in a hug. The hug put him off balance and he wobbled on his heels, almost falling. Romke put one hand on the ground for support and used his other hand to awkwardly pat her back.

"Thank you!" Awbrey said.

Romke patted her shoulder one last time and slid out of her hug, pushing her back. He stood and held out his hand to help her get to her feet. "You can keep an eye on the cornbread and turn it from time to time."

Sophie returned with a bundle of dry branches and fingers stained blue and red. "I found wild berries," she said with a grin. "I had to test them."

Romke gave her a pan to hold the wild blueberries and wild strawberries that she had found. Sophie returned with barely half the pan filled with berries. Those they ate while the chickens roasted and the cornbread almost baked. The berries were so small that they squished between fingers trying to pick them up even with the most delicate touch and they all ended up with stained fingers by the time the pan was empty.

Romke found a piece of tin and bent it into a tent shape. He put it over the cornbread to hold in the heat and allow it to bake. "Don't go touching it with bare fingers now," Romke warned Awbrey.

A cold breeze swept through the campground. Awbrey shivered as the cold air brushed the back of her neck. Everyone felt the coldness in the breeze. All heads rose and twisted, looking to the sky in the direction the breeze had come from. To the east sheet lightning lit the clouds once, then again. The storm was so far away that it was eerie in its silence. There was a beauty in the distant, silent light display in the clouds.

Jaydin tilted his head, listening. Another massive flash of light within the distant mass of high clouds showed the shape of clouds in front of the lightning. In quick succession flash after flash moved through the clouds. Jaydin frowned.

"There should be thunder," Jaydin muttered.

"Too far even for your ears," Romke said, gaze on the eastern sky. "Let's hope it blows itself out before it reaches us. Looks nasty."

"When there is lightning you can tell how far away it is by how long it takes to hear the thunder," Sophie said to Awbrey. "As soon as you see the lightning, start counting until you hear the thunder. Three seconds, three miles. No seconds, it's right on you."

"I know that. Everyone knows that," Awbrey said. Though she did not really. She was not sure what prompted her to lie about such a silly thing and that bugged her as much as Sophie thinking that she did not know anything. Awbrey reached to move the tin tent over the cornbread and burnt her fingers. Fortunately she pulled away fast enough to avoid blisters but her fingertips hurt and turned red.

Sophie pursed her lips. "Did you? Did you really? You looked mighty puzzled at Jaydin."

"I want to go home," Awbrey declared. She stood and faced Romke. "I don't want to be here. I just want to go home."

"See that storm?" Romke asked, pointing at the eastern sky. Sheet lightning flashed again and again, jumping between the clouds silently. "From here we are safe and dry. But that storm is moving. When we hear the thunder it will be upon us. King Eldrid has started a storm. It feels far away now but it is moving towards us. When we hear the thunder from Eldrid's storm it will be too late to find shelter. That thunder will be bad. Very bad. The darkest thunder imaginable."

"But I don't want to be here," Awbrey said in a low, defeated voice.

"Indeed. No one does," Romke said softly.

Everyone was quiet, thinking their own thoughts about the coming storm and what brought them to that moment out in a meadow beside the road while the storm moved in their direction. One of the horses raised its head, studying something in the dim distance. The horse whinnied loudly, its sides heaving. After a moment the horse dropped its head and went back to contentedly grazing.

"Your cornbread smells done," Jaydin said.

The breeze grew into a wind as they finished preparing their meal then ate. The campfire surged and flared against the wind, flames even bending sideways with a loud whoosh a few times. The smell of rain saturated the wind. There was no time to waste on arguing. Their full focus was on finishing the meal and clean up before the storm arrived. The clouds with their flashing sheets of lightning moved closer. By the time they had finished eating and were cleaning the dishes, the low rumble of thunder could be heard.

Sophie wanted to leave the dishes out for the rain to clean but Romke insisted they be cleaned and put away. "They are just going to get wet anyway," Sophie said.

"They'll be a clean wet," Romke said.

They were securely inside the wagon when the first raindrops fell, big, fat globs of water that hit with thuds instead of the pitter-patter of normal rain. Awbrey huddled in the corner of a sofa with a blanket wrapped around her shoulders. Jaydin sat next to her. Romke and Sophie shared the opposite sofa. The wagon felt even smaller than it had before. The metal pots and pans hanging on the wagon side pinged whenever a raindrop hit them.

Romke said, "In the morning we will enter Oakport." Awbrey's interest was caught. Eddy would be in Oakort. If he was not already there then he would be within a day or two. Awbrey listened carefully as Romke continued. "I must pick up another niece. You will wait in the wagon. Keeping out of sight is critical. We don't want people to notice us and remember us when the notices come out. She is a young girl. Maybe twelve. I lose track. She is gifted. Her name is Gemma Diorgal."

"Do you know her talent?" Sophie asked.

"She will have to be the one to tell you," Romke said. "But she is young and talented so it will be necessary to keep a close eye on her, help her rein in her antics."

"Antics?" Sophie asked.

"She likes to use her talent more than she likes to listen to orders not to," Romke said with a shrug.

Awbrey half listened to them talking about their new acquisition to the group. When they reached Oakport she could slip away from the wagon and find Eddy. If he was not already there she would wait for him. No one had to know she left Pindstein with Romke. She did not even know why she had left Pindstein with Romke.

It struck her as odd that Romke knew about this girl in Oakport, knew about Awbrey in Pindstein. Romke had just shown up without warning and her parents had allowed him to drag her away without hesitation.

"How did you know about us?" Awbrey asked, waving her arm at Jaydin and Sophie. "How do you know about this Gemma girl?"

"She is family. Just as you," Romke said.

"Magic runs in the family," Jaydin said when Awbrey stared blankly at Romke.

That information took Awbrey aback. She thought about her family. No one was magic. Then she remembered the night Romke arrived and her mother saying that she had compelled Awbrey to blurt out what Awbrey had seen looking into Romke's eyes. Her mother magic? Awbrey found that hard to believe. She would have seen some sign of it and she had never seen anything to hint that her mother was magic.

"What about my parents?" Awbrey asked. "Are you saying they are magic?"

"Indeed," Romke said.

Her heart caught in her throat. "Why are they not with us if they are magic?" Awbrey asked, leaning forward. "They are in danger if they are magic."

"We felt it wiser to split up," Romke said. "They will go north once they have dispersed their holdings and your brother returns from his business trip."

"Russell? Magic?" Awbrey frowned and sank back on the sofa.

Her brother had never shown any signs of being magic. Awbrey was becoming more and more convinced that this whole thing was a big mistake. Russell was certainly not magic. She still believed that she had no magic talent either.

If they were all magic why had they stayed together and sent her off alone with Romke? It was not fair. If they had to run away from the fear of being arrested for being magic Awbrey would rather be with her parents than in this wagon with strangers.

The storm grew louder and louder as the night wore on. Jaydin and Romke slept on mats between the sofas. Sophie and Awbrey each stretched out on a sofa to sleep. Awbrey could not actually stretch her legs completely straight but lying on her side with her knees bent slightly was comfortable enough. The thunder was so loud that occasionally it made the wagon tremble from the vibration. The lightning lit up the rectangular windows high above the sofas.

It was well into the night before Awbrey fell asleep. The storm had passed, leaving a steady rain that was actually soothing. Awbrey's eyes were heavy and her body longed for sleep yet her brain would not stop working.

If her mother could force people to speak aloud thoughts that they wished to keep unsaid, that was indeed a magic that people would not like to have done to them. Awbrey pictured merchants and customers learning that her mother could compel them to do things that they did not want to do. They would be angry to feel that they had been so used.

Worse even was to imagine her father making people do things. Bad enough to pull words out of someone's mouth but to actually compel people to do things they did not want to do, that was the nightmare people had of magic.

Awbrey had come to realize that her father had told her to go with Romke without any fuss and she had obeyed because he had done something to her, not because she was simply obeying her father. She had not felt the need to resist and ignored it. She had felt nothing at all.

Once Eldrid's new law was posted and people started to think about magic users in their midst would they remember times when near the Tiegs they said or did something they felt they would not normally do? Would they turn her parents over to the authorities to be delivered to King Eldrid? Or would they just burn down the house and hang her parents without taking the time to find out the truth?

What was the truth? Was it magic that she had obeyed or her father's instructions? Was it magic that her mother could get her to blurt out her thoughts? Awbrey did not know.

What Awbrey did know was that she wanted her own soft feather bed with softly scented bedding. Weather permitting, Jane would often hang the pillows outside in the discreetly fenced laundry yard and bring them inside after dinner so that every night when

Awbrey went to bed she was enveloped in the crisp, fresh scent of outside. On cold, rainy days Jane would hang the pillows near the stove so the pillows were warm and cozy when Awbrey went to bed at night.

The wagon, ironically, was outside but smelled of sweating feet, damp wood, and an obnoxious sausage. There was no pillow and the blanket she had to use was a scratchy wool. The slats of wood holding the sofa's cushions could be felt through the thin padding of the cushion. Instead of a soft flannel nightgown stored in a drawer with lavender sachets Awbrey was still wearing the clothing she had been wearing all day.

Dawn brought sunshine and a groggy Awbrey. The ground was wet with puddles from the night's rain storm. When Awbrey walked out into the trees to find privacy her shoes and skirt were soaked wet up to her knees. The skirt acted like a sponge soaking up the water from the tall grasses and undergrowth she walked through. The ground was soaked and the grasses hid puddles that she stepped in several times. Her shoes squished when she walked back to the wagon.

Breakfast that morning was hot only because Romke started a fire for tea. He stabbed four sausages with sticks and laid them in the fire. Sophie dug through the food barrel and found another round of bread while Romke rubbed down the horses and hitched them to the wagon. Jaydin kept a watchful eye on the sausages. Awbrey watched everyone bustle about but did not know what to do, so she just stood watching everyone else work.

Jaydin handed out the sausages on a stick. They were much too hot to eat right away. Jaydin put out the fire by spreading it apart with a stick. He took a bite of the sausage while watching the fire die, grimacing when the bite of steaming sausage burned the inside of his mouth.

"Still needs water," Romke said.

Jaydin nodded. The younger man took another bite of his sausage, gaze on the embers. Romke jerked his head at the wagon. Sophie took Awbrey's arm and pulled her to the back of the wagon.

"What are they doing?" Awbrey asked, craning her neck to look back over her shoulder at the men standing by the dead fire as she followed Sophie. Both men just stood where they were, facing the nearly dead fire.

"They are going to water the embers," Sophie said, pushing Awbrey into the wagon. "You know, their water."

"Oh," Awbrey said, face turning red.

"You are so funny," Sophie said, grinning. "You would think you didn't know that men made water."

Awbrey took a bite of the sausage. Juices ran down her chin and she used her sleeve to wipe her face. Her stomach rumbled in hunger even as she ate the sausage. Sophie broke the bread into quarters and handed a piece to Awbrey. She set the other two pieces down on the stove to give to Romke and Jaydin when they were done taking measures to ensure the fire was completely out.

Awbrey removed her shoes and socks and set them beside the sofa to dry. Jaydin entered the wagon and had barely shut the door when Romke released the brake. The wagon rocked a bit before lurching forward. Jaydin sat on the sofa and studied Awbrey. He did not even notice the bread until Sophie picked up a piece and handed it to him.

"So if I tell you my dreams can you tell my future?" Jaydin asked Awbrey.

"No," Awbrey said. "I told you, it's your dream. Dreams use symbols and I've learned the symbols is all. I can only tell you what it means."

Jaydin nodded. "I had a dream that Eldrid's men rode in the storm. Wherever they landed houses burst into flame. I could see my mother, surrounded by flame. A dove the size of an owl plucked her out of the flames. They rose into the storm and away from the flames. One of Eldrid's men spotted her and started shouting. They all started shooting arrows at her and the bird dropped her. That is when I woke."

"It's from what Romke said last night," Awbrey said. "You held onto the thought that the new law will bring a storm. Your mother will be caught in the storm coming. Is your mother a shape shifter? Perhaps a young sister? She will try to help your mother without caring who sees what she is. At least that's your fear." Awbrey took a deep breath. The answers came so quickly to her now that she did not even have to give it much thought.

"It already happened," Sophie said. "It was the sister the archers shot."

"I don't understand," Awbrey said.

"Two nights before King Eldrid made his law I had that dream," Jaydin said. "It was my mother they went to arrest. My sister decided to distract them so my mother could escape. They are both sitting in the cells beneath the castle. My mother would not leave my sister."

"Your sister turns into a dove?" Awbrey asked.

"In the dream. In reality she turned into a mountain lion. Poor choice," Jaydin said with a shrug.

Awbrey stared at Jaydin, eyes wide, mouth slightly open. Shape shifters were a myth. Jaydin had said that he was a shape shifter but Awbrey still found it difficult to believe. Now he was saying there were more shape shifters.

"Wait. I thought the law won't be posted yet," Awbrey said. "Isn't that what Romke said? That we are racing to get away before the new law is announced?"

"It was already known in Lethbridge. It's announcing it to the rest of the country that will take time. He will send runners across the rest of the kingdom once he is prepared."

"Why did the baron want to arrest your mother?" Awbrey asked.

"It was common knowledge that she is magic," Jaydin said. "She never hid it."

"Baron Barnett grabbed everyone in Lethbridge who was known to be magic," Sophie said. "Jaydin's mother was the first one but several others were taken that same day."

"Shape shifters living right in the capitol," Awbrey said in amazement. The very idea of shape shifters was so difficult to believe, that they lived and moved about Lethbridge stunned Awbrey.

"Not all were shape shifters," Sophie said. "Jaydin and his sister are the only changers in the city."

"What about his mother?" Awbrey asked Sophie.

"She made plants grow," Jaydin said. He smiled as he thought of his mother. It was a sad smile. "And she can keep produce from spoiling."

Awbrey frowned. "Why would she be arrested for that? Keeping fruit from spoiling seems a wonderful talent."

"Baron Barnett feels it interferes with destiny. All magic disrupts destiny," Sophie said. Awbrey stared at Sophie. "Baron Barnett feels our lives follow a destiny and by using magic that destiny is disrupted."

"You said that before. Wouldn't using magic be part of destiny then?" Awbrey asked. She wrinkled her nose as she rode that thought in a circle.

"Imagine how he feels about girls who can see the future and use that knowledge?" Sophie asked, leaning toward Awbrey.

Awbrey pulled back, shrinking into the corner of the sofa. One of the reasons she had never told anyone of her impressions when she looked into people's eyes was because they were just fleeting impressions. Sometimes, like with Romke, she could see for a moment specific things happening but it all went so fast. There was no changing what she saw. The dreams were slightly different. The dreams were people's own. The dreams gave people warnings that they missed during their conscious moments so they could prepare for what was to come.

"You are scaring her," Jaydin said to Sophie.

"I don't see the future," Awbrey said softly.

"She should be scared," Sophie said in a hard tone.

"I don't see the future," Awbrey said again, louder.

"It's what Baron Barnett believes that matters," Sophie said.

The wagon rattled and swayed for only a few hours before stopping. Romke opened the back door, telling them to stretch their legs before they entered Oakport. Awbrey put her damp shoes and socks back on before leaving the wagon. Rooftops were visible in the distance because they stood on a hill. Awbrey walked down the road toward the town, Romke falling into step beside her. She did not go too far, just as far as the lead horse.

"Oakport. Eddy said he could come home once a month. That's such a long trip," Awbrey said. "It would take a whole day."

"The wagon takes longer," Rome said, following her gaze to the distant city. "On horseback he could do it in half a day and return on the river."

"Who is Eddy?" Sophie asked.

Awbrey looked back at the girl, not having heard her follow

them. Awbrey did not reply. Romke said, "The girl's betrothed."

"Not betrothed," Awbrey said to Romke. "We were to be married next year. In April when the tulips were in bloom. But now I won't be home to wed."

The idea of not marrying Eddy brought tears to her eyes and the words caught in her throat. Awbrey knew that it was her destiny to marry Eddy. She knew with certainty. It was this mysterious Baron Barnett who broke her destiny and sent her life spiraling out of control. Awbrey wished she could make this Baron Barnett illegal so that he could be arrested and removed from ruining her destiny.

"Your Eddy is in the town ahead?" Sophie asked in interest.

Awbrey shook her head. It was difficult to ignore Sophie. "I don't know. He was still in Pindstein when we left. I didn't even get to say good-bye."

Sophie patted Awbrey's shoulder in sympathy. "I didn't know you left a betrothed."

Awbrey resisted the urge to shrug away Sophie's hand. The frail, blonde girl was trying to be nice but Awbrey was not feeling receptive to being comforted. Awbrey stared down the road at the town in the distance lost in her misery. The break was brief and Romke shuffled them back into the wagon. Before long the wagon swayed and bounced along the road.

When they arrived in Oakport Romke stuck his head into the back of the wagon through the shuttered opening. "Stay inside the wagon, mind you. I don't know how long I'll be. Maybe an hour.

Maybe four."

Once again Awbrey retreated into her own thoughts. Being in Oakport filled her with mixed emotions. Being so close yet so far made her miss Eddy so deeply that it hurt. Eddy could be riding right past the wagon that very moment on his way to start his apprenticeship with Jacksol, oblivious to the fact that she was inside the wagon and she would never know.

Another thread of logic had started to override Awbrey's thoughts of slipping out of the wagon and staying with Eddy in Oakport. If Awbrey stayed with Eddy she could be putting Eddy in danger. If he was with her and she was arrested he would be arrested as well. Though she was not magic, everyone else seemed to think she was. Awbrey writhed at how unfair it was. She had done nothing wrong.

Gradually Awbrey became aware of a noisy commotion outside the wagon. Jaydin and Sophie were both trying to peer out the window without being seen. A man was shouting and a child's voice wailed in protest. Whatever Sophie saw made her eyes widen and cover her mouth with her fist in horror.

"What is it?" Awbrey asked.

"That poor boy," Sophie whispered.

Awbrey stepped up on the sofa between them and peered out. A tall, heavyset man holding a club was standing over a small figure on the ground. A crowd gathered but held back as the man swung his club at anyone who dared approach. Satisfied that no one would interfere, the man reached down and grabbed a handful of the child's shirt. He pulled the boy to his feet, shaking the boy so hard that the boy swung about like a rag doll.

Awbrey's ire rose. She was not about to let some bully beat a helpless child. First she hurried to the door at the back of the wagon and tried to open it but it was locked. Awbrey immediately turned and spotted the small shuttered opening at the front of the wagon. Awbrey pried open the shutters with her fingertips, pushing as hard as she could and then pulling her hands apart until the shutter slid apart slightly. She repeated the process until she had a gap large enough to fit her hand through and could use her palm on the edge of the shutter door to push it into its recessed track.

As soon as Awbrey had the shutters open she climbed onto the stove and dove head first through the opening. It was a tight squeeze and her skirt was too bulky with fabric so she got stuck. Awbrey twisted and pulled on the fabric of her skirt. She tugged sections at a time desperately to free herself. When she pulled enough fabric through the opening to give her legs room she fell onto the driver's bench, landing on her shoulder. Awbrey heard Sophie calling her name but ignored the frail, blonde girl.

Though it felt like time crawled, Awbrey managed to escape the wagon in just a matter of minutes. She immediately ran to the boy's aid, putting her body between the angry man and the boy lying on the dusty street. The man stared at Awbrey in surprise then raised his club threateningly.

"Get outa ma way," the man yelled.

He was a large man and towered above Awbrey. Morning stubble covered the bottom half of his face. He smelled so strongly of sweat that Awbrey's nose twitched. Perspiration dampened his shirt under his arms and down his back. Many of his teeth were missing and the rest that were visible were stained brown with black spots. The stubble on his face was gray but the hair on his head was a faded orange.

"He's just a child," Awbrey said in a calm voice.

Awbrey faced the man when he raised his club above his shoulder. No thoughts of backing down entered her mind. Awbrey would not stand by and watch a child being beaten. Some of the gathered watchers called out warnings to her. Apparently the man was well known in Oakport and there was genuine concern that she would be hurt if she interfered. Yet no one stepped up to help her protect the young boy.

"He deserves his whipping," the man said.

"You will not hurt this child," Awbrey said, facing him with arms crossed in front of her chest.

"Move out of my way, girl!" the man warned.

Chapter Five

Awbrey turned her back to the man, eliciting several gasps from the gathered crowd. The boy was only about seven or eight years old. He was sitting up now. He was an attractive boy with big brown eyes and thick eyelashes lining his eyelids. Tousled dirty blonde hair covered his head, cropped short on the sides but allowed to grow several inches long along his crown. The boy used his sleeve to wipe blood from a scratch on his chin. A big scrape on his cheek did not bleed but had gravel stuck to the wound.

"Run home, boy," Awbrey said gently to the boy.

The boy just sat where he was on the street, staring at her in surprise. Suddenly his eyes widened at something he saw behind her. He scrambled to his feet and vanished into the crowd at a run. Awbrey turned. Two men now blocked the angry man's access to Awbrey. A third man also stepped out of the crowd and put his hand on the club.

The angry man shrugged off the man's hold but he lowered the club. He glared at Awbrey, looked at each of the men between him and the girl, and stalked away. Taking on three adult men was a different story than taking on a child and a girl. Awbrey thanked the men for their assistance, resisting the urge to point out that they could have helped the boy instead of waiting to give aid until she was the one threatened.

"That was very brave and very foolish, girl," one of the men said. He looked uncomfortable, glancing around constantly.

"He was hurting a child," Awbrey said.

"It was his own brat," the man said, shaking his head.

"C'mon," Sophie said, grabbing Awbrey's arm and tugging.

"He was hurting a child," Awbrey said, digging in her heels. "No one hurts a child."

"You heard the man. It was his own child," Sophie said.

"That is even worse! I told the boy to go home. If he goes home this man will just beat him there. We must find him," Awbrey said, looking in the direction the boy had taken and vanished.

"We must get back in the wagon," Sophie insisted. "I am sure his mother will protect him."

Awbrey's urge to find the boy gradually faded. His mother would protect him. Awbrey allowed Sophie to turn her to the wagon.

A large wolf stood near the wagon door. The animal whined then jumped into the wagon through the open door. Awbrey dug in her heels when Sophie tried dragging her to the wagon with a large wolf inside. Sophie glanced nervously around them. The crowd had already mostly dispersed. Luckily no one was near the rear of the wagon to notice the wolf. Everyone had gathered near the front of the wagon and moved away in that direction as well.

"It's Jaydin," Sophie hissed. "Get inside."

Jaydin poked his head out of the wagon door and gestured for them to hurry. Awbrey still hesitated. Romke came up behind them.

"What's this?" Romke asked, a hint of anger in his voice.

Awbrey looked over her shoulder when she heard Romke speak. Romke carried a satchel in his left hand and held the hand of a young girl with his right hand. The girl wore a crisp blue dress that stopped just above her ankles. She wore white leather button-up boots and lace edged socks. The girl also wore a wide-brimmed straw hat with a ribbon around the crown that matched her dress. The hat hid her face as she stood next to Romke staring at her feet.

"He was hurting a child," Awbrey said.

Romke looked around at the departing crowd and nodded. Romke looked up at Jaydin peering out of the wagon with no shirt on. Jaydin looked guilty and ducked back inside the wagon. Romke sighed.

"I am guessing no one saw a large carnivore appear in the middle of the town or things wouldn't be so calm now," Romke said. He passed the girl's hand to Awbrey. "Take her inside, girl."

"There's a wolf," Awbrey said.

"Wolf?" the girl asked, looking up in interest.

"Big blue eyes framed by black lashes were the first thing Awbrey noticed about the girl's face. Freckles dotted the girl's cheeks and across her nose. The girl smiled, showing white teeth with a slight overbite. Awbrey smiled at the girl and crouched down next to her.

"Hello. My name is Awbrey," Awbrey said.

"Hello. I am Gemma," the girl said.

"Inside. Inside," Romke said.

"But I want to see a wolf," Gemma protested sweetly.

"There is no wolf," Romke said.

"Oh," Gemma said in disappointment. The girl hung her head again and patiently stood frozen, holding Awbrey's hand.

"She reminds me of my cousin's mechanical wind-up bird," Sophie said in a dry tone.

"Inside," Romke said. The added edge to his voice sent them scurrying through the wagon door.

Jaydin was wearing a shirt by the time they entered the wagon. He sat on a sofa quietly, averting his gaze as he buttoned up the last few buttons on his shirt. Romke gave Jaydin a hard look but did not say anything. Romke shut the door and soon the wagon was swaying on its way out of Oakport. Awbrey watched the rooftops pass until only blue sky was visible through the window.

"You can take off your hat, Gemma," Sophie said, watching the girl sit rigidly on the sofa next to Awbrey, head still down.

Gemma obediently reached up and removed the hat. The girl looked around the wagon in interest, hat in hand. Mousy brown hair was plaited neatly into braids on each side of her face. Her forehead was broad. Awbrey tilted her head as she looked at the girl. She looked familiar yet Awbrey knew she had never met the girl before.

"What is your talent?" Jaydin asked.

"I can sing," Gemma said in her sweet voice.

Sophie sucked in her breath. "Not in here, child."

"What is it?" Jaydin asked.

"She has the power to shatter stone with a song," Sophie said.

"You are much younger than Romke thought," Awbrey said, frowning at Sophie. "How old are you, Gemma?"

"That's rude," Gemma said. "You shouldn't ask a woman her age."

"Women, no. But everyone asks children their age," Jaydin said.

"Not me. Do you sing, too?" Gemma said.

"Not very well," Jaydin said. He smiled at a memory. "People groan and cover their ears when I sing."

"Me, too!" Gemma said in excitement. She looked around the wagon again. "I was hoping to see a wolf. Are you the wolf?"

"I am Jaydin. This is Sophie. Awbrey is sitting next to you."

"I know who Awbrey is. And Uncle Romke. You forgot Uncle Romke," Gemma said. "And the boy. Did you see the wolf, boy?"

Gemma looked at the pile of luggage and blankets in the corner. Everyone followed her gaze. Gemma tilted her head. "Maybe he fell asleep," Gemma said.

"There's no one there," Sophie said.

"I think he saw a wolf," Gemma said.

Awbrey wondered if Gemma was all right in the head. She exchanged glances with Jaydin. The man shrugged, clearly wondering the same thing as he looked at the odd little girl. Gemma did not even look like she had reached her tenth birthday yet. Her behavior was also quite odd. Awbrey had heard of children having make-believe friends but they were usually younger children.

"That was foolish," Sophie said to Jaydin. He looked across to her in surprise. "Changing," Sophie said to be clear. Jaydin got a sheepish look on his face and averted his gaze again.

"I thought he was about to bash her skull in with that club," Jaydin said. "It all happened so fast. I had just stepped out when those men moved into position between her and the club. It was like someone moved them. They just slid into place. I swear their feet did not move. And the club just froze. For just a second. Just long enough for the men to be in place."

"Men cannot ignore a pretty girl in distress," Sophie said.

"You think I'm pretty?" Awbrey asked, mood perking up. It was always nice to hear.

"I think you were very brave. You stood up to a man wielding a club. A very big, angry man," Sophie said.

"He was hurting a child," Awbrey said. She did not feel brave. If someone hurt a child stopping that someone was all she thought of. Anything else left her brain.

"Very brave but very stupid. Very, very stupid," Sophie muttered. Awbrey frowned at Sophie.

"Are you the wolf?" Gemma asked again.

"Yes, child. I am a shape shifter. Sophie talks to animals and

Awbrey sees the future."

"I do not," Awbrey said.

"You aren't supposed to tell other's talents," Sophie scolded Jaydin at the same time.

Awbrey turned to Gemma, intending to explain the difference between seeing the future and simply getting impressions from people. When Awbrey looked into Gemma's eyes she forgot what she was about to say. Gemma brought danger. It was not Gemma herself. It just seemed to follow her. Wherever Gemma went there would be trouble. Awbrey frowned.

"What do you see?" Sophie asked.

Awbrey looked up from Gemma to Sophie, words on her lips to dispute that she had seen anything. The sun behind Sophie made her hair glow. Sparkles danced above Sophie's head like diamonds in a crown. Awbrey knew that Sophie had to be Princess Sophie though the other girl denied it.

The impression always came to Awbrey. She had no control. What if she tried to see something on purpose? Awbrey concentrated, willing herself to see Sophie's future. Nothing came to her. Trees blocked the sun and even the inadvertent crown of light winked out of sight. It was not a real impression. The images had not struck Awbrey from looking into Sophie's eyes. It had merely been a trick of the eye from sunshine hitting the frail, blonde girl just right.

"The sun gave you a crown," Awbrey said to Sophie.

The frail, blonde girl looked uncomfortable for a moment, gaze dropping away as she frowned. Then she smiled and looked up at Awbrey. "Are you saying I'll meet a prince?"

Awbrey shook her head. "No. I don't think you need a prince to wear a crown. It was just a trick of the light anyway."

"Tell her," Jaydin said.

Sophie shook her head. "There's nothing to tell." Sophie turned to Gemma. "You are a Diorgil, so you must be a descendant of Romke's sister. The youngest one. June."

"Gramma June was my mom's mom's mom," Gemma said. "I remember her. She left us two winters ago. Mom says left us. I know she died. Gramma June could sing like me. Before she died we would sing together. Her favorite song was the Flower Dance song. Do you know the Flower Dance song?"

"I do not," Sophie said. Jaydin and Awbrey shook their heads no.

"I can sing it for you," Gemma said. She bounced up and down on her seat. "When Gramma June sang it the flowers would glow. I can't make the flowers glow. But I can make them do other things."

"Let's wait," Sophie said, shifting her weight in discomfort at the idea. "When we stop next we'll ask Romke if you can sing the Flower Song. Besides, we don't have any flowers."

Gemma stuck her lower lip out in a pout. "He already said no singing until we get to where we're going."

"Well, there you have it," Sophie said, relieved. She relaxed. "No singing until we get to where we're going."

"But I like to sing," Gemma said. "Mama let me sing the Flower Song every morning. She said a fish must swim."

"It is hard," Jaydin said. "Sometimes my muscles ache when I go a long time without changing shape. It's like I'm stuck in a box where I can't stand straight or stretch out lying down."

"I never met a shape shifter before," Gemma said. "What can you be? How long can you be it? Can you talk when you are an animal?"

Jaydin grinned. "The wolf and bear are the easiest. Once I was a goat."

"Could you be a pony? I could ride you. I'd call you Flower," Gemma said, bouncing up and down on her seat again in excitement.

"I was a pony once," Jaydin said. "I can stay in the shape for days but after a while I get confused. I normally don't go past a day. No, I can't talk when I'm a wolf because wolves can't talk."

"Can you change into other people?" Gemma asked in a low voice.

"That's forbidden," Jaydin said, cheeks flushing.

"But you could if you wanted?" Gemma asked, eyes widening. "Could you look just like me?"

"What do you mean you get confused?" Sophie asked.

"It's like you become the animal. Think like the animal. It takes great effort to maintain your own identity when shifted," Jaydin said.

The discussion made Awbrey uncomfortable. Listening to them talk so casually about shape shifting twisted her stomach into knots.

Awbrey had seen the wolf and knew that Jaydin really could change. It felt wrong somehow.

Awbrey did not understand why it bothered her but it did. She liked Jaydin. He was a nice man, polite and pleasant. She felt comfortable around him. Yet when she looked at him and thought about him turning into a wolf it made her insides squirm. As long as she did not think about what he did she was fine with him.

It was well into afternoon when Romke stopped the wagon for a break and to eat the midday meal. Jaydin devoured a whole loaf of bread before Romke even dug out the food packages from the barrel on the side of the wagon. It was the first time Romke had stopped on the side of the road instead of finding a place to pull the wagon out of sight.

"It's the change. It takes so much energy that he is starving," Sophie said, noticing Awbrey's wide eyes as she watched Jaydin eat.

Romke handed out cheese wedges, apples, carrots, and thick slices of ham. "Now, what happened in Oakport?"

"A man was beating a boy with a club," Jaydin said around a mouthful of food. "Awbrey saved the boy."

"Did you actually see him use the club?" Romke asked.

"He struck him several times. The club would have severely hurt the boy. Likely killed him. I did not wait to see him use the club," Awbrey said.

"Something strange happened," Jaydin said.

"Indeed," Romke said, gaze still on Awbrey.

"When Awbrey had her back to the man with the club, he raised it, like he was going to hit her. For just a moment the club froze in the air. At first I thought I imagined it but I saw the man's eyes when it happened and he noticed it also. Then two men slid between Awbrey and the club," Jaydin said.

Romke looked around the group, frowning. "Indeed."

"Is that the boy in the wagon?" Gemma asked.

Romke frowned. He ducked inside the wagon and returned holding a boy firmly by the boy's shirt collar. It was indeed the boy who Awbrey had saved from a clubbing. Romke shook the boy just enough to make the boy squirm on his tiptoes.

Awbrey watched in amazement at how roughly Romke handled the boy. The boy was not in any danger from Romke yet she still did not like that Romke had to be so firm. The boy had done nothing wrong, except hide away in the wagon. Awbrey resisted the urge to tell Romke to be more gentle in his handling of the boy.

"I could sing the Flower Dance song," Gemma suggested.

"No," Romke said to Gemma. He looked back to the boy and shook him again. "Was the plan to rob us, boy?"

"No, sir," the boy said. Despite his position he did not look frightened at all. He pointed his finger at Awbrey. "She said to go home. But if I went home my pa would beat me even more."

"Beat you even more? Because you failed to rob us?" Romke asked.

"No, sir," the boy said. He sniffed the air. "I'm so starved. Mind if I have a bit of that cheese? I s'ppose that ham is all gone? It smells mighty fine."

"He's just a boy," Awbrey said, unable to withstand the boy's torture any longer.

"It's common to create a commotion in order to rob travelers while they are distracted," Romke said to Awbrey. "Boy, what happened to set your da on you?"

"Nothing, sir," the boy said, dropping his gaze. He wiped his nose with the back of his hand. "I just fell asleep, is all. I'm s'posed to bring in the firewood."

Romke released the boy, glaring at him. The boy rubbed his shoulder where Romke had been holding his shirt but otherwise did not move. Romke sliced some cheese from the round and held it out. The boy ate the cheese faster than Jaydin could have. Romke tossed him an apple. The boy grabbed it deftly out of the air and within a minute he held nothing but the stem. He had eaten the apple core and all. Romke sighed and cut off another slice of ham and gave that to the boy as well.

"I can't take you back. I can't leave you here," Romke said, watching the boy take a bite of ham, closing his eyes as he slowly chewed the meat. "What am I to do with you, eh?"

The boy swallowed. "I don't mind going to where it is you're going," the boy said. "I never seen a shape shifters and I sure want to hear the Flower Dance song." He took another bite of ham, savoring the bite.

"He heard us talking," Sophie said. "Are you magic, boy? Were you invisible?"

"Name's Tucker. I'm just good at hiding. Hide a lot."

Gemma was humming. Romke ordered her to silence. Gemma scowled but stopped. "Tucker wants to hear the Flower Dance song."

"Tucker has to wait," Romke said. "Everyone, stretch your legs for ten minutes. Do your nature calls. We aren't stopping again until dark. Sophie, watch Gemma."

"Of course," Sophie said sweetly.

Romke was unhappy. He stared back down the road in the direction they had come then shook his head as he turned to Tucker. The boy's eyes grew wide and he straightened as he faced Romke. The older man stared at Tucker thoughtfully, muttering under his breath about foolish children then walked up to the horses to check on them.

Awbrey walked toward the trees lining the road, keeping an eye on where Jaydin went. She always watched where Jaydin headed to make his nature call before going in the opposite direction. Jaydin ducked into the trees on the east side of the road. Awbrey headed into the trees on the west side. Sophie and Gemma entered the trees on the same side of the road as Awbrey headed but they walked past the wagon and up past the horses before ducking into the trees and undergrowth. Awbrey was back by the rear of the wagon when she stepped into the trees.

The undergrowth was sparse between the trees near the road and

Awbrey had to work her way deeper into the trees before she felt there was enough coverage to prevent anyone from the road seeing her. Awbrey picked a spot that was fairly level without thistles or cockleburs growing near, trampling the grass down by stepping on it. It had not taken her long to learn that she did not like grass tickling parts best left covered but exposed when needing to heed nature in nature.

Awbrey straightened after taking care of her business. As she adjusted her skirt she noticed that the hem was already looking quite dirty and wrinkled. She had been wearing the dress since leaving home. Awbrey raised her arm and smelled her armpits. No unpleasant aroma assaulted her nose. Yet.

An acorn dropped to the ground right in front of her. A second acorn hit her shoe. Awbrey looked up into the trees above her, expecting to see a troublesome squirrel. What she saw was Eddy. At first she could not believe her eyes. Eddy had climbed halfway up the tree and hung over a branch, grinning at her.

"Eddy!"

"Shh," he hissed, holding his finger to his lips.

Eddy climbed down the tree smoothly, without hesitation, dropping the last few feet to the ground. He always made physical endeavors look easy. Awbrey ran into his arms. Eddy wrapped his arms around her and gave her a strong hug. She had never been so happy to see anyone in her entire life.

Her Eddy was right there, in the flesh. Relief and joy and a feeling that all was right in the world filled her. Then Awbrey realized that Eddy had been up in the tree above her, looking down at her as she squatted to take care of very private business. Awbrey pulled back and slapped his arm.

"You saw me doing my business!"

"I saw nothing, Awbrey" Eddy said, pulling her back into his arms.

"You saw that I was taking care of my business," Awbrey insisted. Worse, Awbrey realized that he had seen her smelling her armpits.

"Oh, Awbrey, it doesn't matter. Everyone heeds the call of nature. You know that, right? I have to relieve myself every day. Multiple times a day. It's not a deep, dark secret."

"It's still, well, embarrassing," Awbrey said, cheeks flaring red.

"I had to be sure you were alone," Eddy said.

"Did you follow us from Oakport? Are you here to take me home? Please take me home, Eddy" Awbrey said.

"I've been following you from Pindstein," Eddy said.

"Pindstein?" Why didn't you let me know sooner?" Awbrey asked.

"I tried but it wasn't easy." Eddy stroked her hair. Awbrey laid her head on his chest.

"But why are you hiding?" Awbrey asked.

"I had to figure out what to do. I almost had a heart attack when you faced that man with a club. Don't ever do that again!"

"You saw that? He was hurting a child," Awbrey said.

Eddy kissed the top of her head. "Yes. I understand. Sensible fear flees you when that happens. But try to be afraid enough to not step in front of an angry man wielding a club. I couldn't get to you. I thought that man would crack your skull and I couldn't get to you."

"I'm sorry for scaring you," Awbrey said.

Awbrey leaned her head back to look up at him. She put her palm on his cheek. Her heart was so filled with joy at seeing his face. Eddy put his hand on her hand on his face. They stood for several minutes, content to be in each other's arms for a few minutes. Awbrey sighed when reality intruded on their private moment.

"Don't you have to stay in Oakport? Did you come to say good-bye?" Awbrey asked, voice catching.

"I don't know what's going to happen, Awbrey," Eddy said. "Everything has changed. That new law has changed everything. Do you understand what that means?"

Awbrey rested her cheek on Eddy's chest, listening to his heart beating. Hearing the steady thump of his heart under her cheek always relaxed her. Normally it relaxed her. That time it reminded her that time was limited.

She raised her head to look up at Eddy. "I want to go home. So badly. But I'm coming to realize that's not a choice any longer. They are all magic, Eddy. They think I am magic even though I'm not. I'm really not. But they think I am and that's what matters. If you are with us you will be arrested just the same as us. Is that what you mean? That now I am going to be illegal?"

"No, Awbrey, it has nothing to do with you. Well, I suppose in a way it does. Listen for a minute. If it was me, if I was magic and you weren't would you still want to marry me?" Eddy asked.

"That's silly. Of course I would," Awbrey said without hesitation. "In a year. When I am eighteen and the tulips are in bloom. If you were magic it wouldn't matter to me at all."

"I believe you," Eddy said with small smile.

"That's because it's true," Awbrey said.

"There's something I have to tell you, Awbrey," Eddy said. He smiled down at her and kissed the tip of her nose. "Do you love me?"

"More than the moon and stars," Awbrey said. She sighed and pulled out of his embrace. "I love you more than anything. I thought you knew. I love you so much that I have to say farewell because as long as you are around me you are in danger."

"You don't put me in danger," Eddy said.

"I do. And because of that you must go. Go now," Awbrey said, tears running down her cheeks. Even though she was telling him to go she was gripping his shirt in her fists.

"Do you think I would want any less than you?" Eddy asked. "If you were magic and I wasn't it would not be as important to me as having you with me, Awbrey."

"But I don't want you to be in danger, Eddy," Awbrey said.

"Always so dramatic," Eddy said.

"I am not," Awbrey protested, voice rising. "Eddard Simpson, you take that back. It is not being dramatic to want to keep you safe."

Eddy sighed. "I'm sorry, darling Awbrey. I can see it in your eyes, that fire. That same fire that sends you into the melee when you are overcome with the need to protect."

The sound of several riders on the road caught their attention. "Shh," Eddy whispered, crouching and pulling Awbrey down with him. Awbrey squirmed when a thistle brushed her leg under her skirt. Eddy gave her a warning glance but she could not ignore the sharp spines of the thistle on bare skin. She stayed in a crouch but moved away from the thistle. Eddy moved next to her.

The horses slowed and stopped at the wagon. Together they stood but kept their backs bent and moved from tree to tree towards the wagon on the road. They stayed low and wound their way through the trees closer and closer to the road until they could see the wagon but remain hidden from view. One man was clearly visible, framed by tree branches.

"The boy's father," Eddy whispered.

Awbrey had recognized the man immediately. The angry man sat on a horse, three mounted men fanned out behind him. He rode with three other men just as large and rough looking as him. One of the men even wore an eye patch with thick scars visible from the patch up to his forehead. Romke stood at the rear of the wagon. He faced the riders with his arms crossed in front of his chest. There was no sign of Tucker.

Chapter Six

"You owe me, old man," Tucker's father said. "The boy's run off and I didn't get your gold in town."

"Gold? What makes you think I have any gold?" Rome asked.

"Wagon like that. You carry your gold with you," the man said. "Hand it over and I'll let you live."

"No," Romke said, shaking his head.

"No," the man repeated.

"Even if I had any gold I wouldn't hand it over to a bully who beats children," Romke said. "A man who beats defenseless children. Tch."

"The boy's just a street urchin. I took him in. I fed him. I gave him a trade. When he disobeys I have the right to discipline him," the man said, face flushing a deep red in anger. He dismounted, facing Romke with his club in one hand, softly striking the palm of his other hand with the club. "I'm sorta glad you won't cooperate. I have the need to bash a skull. When I'm done with you I'll get my hands on that little bitch who made a fool of me."

Eddy's eyes narrowed when he heard the man threaten Awbrey. He started to stand but Awbrey put her hand on his arm and shook his head. "Wait," she whispered. "He might be full of bluster. If you show yourself he might feel threatened."

"He should feel threatened," Eddy said in a low voice but he waited.

The men with Tucker's father were still mounted. Their horses were growing agitated. The men turned their attention from Romke to trying to control their horses. Even from the cover of the trees Awbrey could see the whites of one of the horse's eyes. Something was scaring the horses. Tucker's father looked behind him, frowned, and grabbed his horse's reins.

A growl then a roar came from the trees on the other side of the road, the east side of the road. Tucker's father's horse tried to bolt and the man held tight to the reins as the horse half reared. The angry man drew blood on the horse's tender mouth as he used his body weight on the bit between the horse's teeth to drag the horse's head back down.

A bear ambled out onto the road, between the horses and Oakport. It paused, sniffing the air, swinging its head from side to side. The horses were all whinnying in panic. The three horses hitched to the wagon tossed their heads and took a step or two but otherwise remained calm. The bear took a few shuffling steps closer to the horses, still sniffing the air.

"Stay here," Eddy said to Awbrey.

Even as Eddy spoke he was moving. Awbrey grabbed at his sleeve but missed. Eddy ran nimbly between the trees toward the wagon. Awbrey followed Eddy, trying to stay low yet run as fast as she could. Her skirts caught in dead branch half buried in the ground and she had to stop and untangle it. It only took a moment but she lost sight of Eddy.

Awbrey hurried closer to the road to get a better view but she stayed within the safety of the trees. She could see Eddy just ahead of her and stopped in her tracks. Eddy boldly walked out of the trees next to the road, stopping in the grass lining the road. He stood between the horses and the bear but on the side.

Awbrey crouched next to a tree, wrapping her arm around the tree trunk. She had to push down some underbrush in front of her face to get a clear view of Eddy and the riders at the rear of the wagon. Her heart raced in her chest.

Romke still stood in place by the rear of the wagon, watching the whole thing without any expression on his face. The bear saw Eddy and growled but did not move any closer. The horses were struggling against their riders, whinnying in alarm and turning in circles. The gang of thieves swore and tried to gain control of their mounts.

Tucker's foster father swore at his horse as it continuously threw its head back, the whites of its eyes showing. Romke watched it all without moving a muscle. If he saw Eddy on the side of the road he gave no sign of it. The older man simply stood with his arms crossed, watching the commotion.

The crazed horse managed to break free of the angry man's grip.

The animal ran in the opposite direction of the bear on the road, past the wagon. It had not gotten very far past the wagon when it suddenly stopped in the middle of the road. The horse stood, legs splayed, head down, and sides heaving.

Tucker's foster father growled in rage, his attention back on Romke. He advanced on the older man. He pulled his club wielding arm back, almost like drawing a bow, twisting his body to put as much force as possible into the swing. He raised the club, aiming for Romke's head. The club froze in mid-swing. The club hung in the air unmoving. The angry man had not frozen though and he yelped in pain when his muscles kept pushing against the club frozen in place. It was a miracle he did not dislocate his shoulder.

Romke had not even flinched though he had taken a step to his left, effectively putting himself out of reach of the club if it had not frozen in place. Romke's eyebrows rose as he studied the club hanging in the air just above him. The bear gave a yelp and ran off the road into the trees, vanishing as he crashed through the underbrush.

Seeing the club handing immobile in midair was the limit for the rest of the gang of thieves. With the bear gone the road was clear for an escape. They yelled at Tucker's foster father to let it go but he ignored their pleas to give up. He gripped the club with both hands and pushed and pulled with all his might. The club did not move even a hair's width.

The bear reappeared, coming out of the trees closer to the

wagon. The other riders let their horses have free rein and all raced away at a full gallop back in the direction of Oakport. Hearing his companions flee, the angry man looked over his shoulder at the departing riders. His rage faded. Tucker's foster father looked at the approaching bear and back up at the club hanging in the air and visibly deflated.

"You may have won this time, old man, but if I ever see you again you will pay," the angry man said.

Tucker's foster father ran to his terrified horse and leaped into the saddle. He turned the horse to face the direction of Oakport and kicked him into a gallop after his companions. The horse swung to the very edge of the road as it raced past the wagon, causing Eddy to duck back to avoid being struck. Romke reached up and grabbed the club. The piece of wood fell into his hand. Romke tossed the club in the air and caught it a few times then tossed it aside, gaze on Eddy now.

Awbrey hurried out of the trees lining the road. Sophie and Gemma emerged as well. They had been relatively close to Awbrey but she had not even known they were there. The bear lumbered away. A few minutes later Jaydin emerged, still in the process of dressing. His shirt was unbuttoned and he carried his boots. Sophie looked at Eddy with interest.

"Indeed," Romke said. He looked down the road back to Oakport. "It could have been worse. But not much. I have told you not to do anything to draw attention to your talents. I have faced worse than four petty thieves before. The bear could be a coincidence. An unmoving club is pretty clear cut magic."

"Sophie wouldn't let me sing," Gemma complained. "I wanted to sing the Fireworks song but she wouldn't let me."

Romke's head jerked back in surprise. "It wasn't you? I thought the club was you."

Awbrey stood next to Eddy and put her hand in his. What a relief that no one had been hurt. "Where is Tucker?"

"Hiding," Romke said. Romke stuck his head through the wagon's door. "You can come out, boy." Romke looked at Eddy. "If you have big dreams of taking her home, forget it, boy."

"I know. It isn't safe any longer. I am joining you," Eddy announced with his ready smile.

Romke shook his head. "Not wise. It was already dangerous. Now we are exposed." Tucker bounded out of the wagon. "And now we're collecting extras left and right."

Awbrey felt overjoyed at hearing that Eddy planned on joining the group. As long as Eddy was at her side everything was all right. A great weight lifted off her shoulders. With Eddy she was ready to face anything that came their way.

"What about your apprenticeship?" Romke asked.

"It wouldn't have worked," Eddy said.

"Indeed," Romke said slowly, eyes narrowing as he studied Eddy. "There are risks in joining this merry group. The plan was to let you know once we were settled, let you make your decisions when the dust stopped flying around."

"This dust doesn't need to settle for me to know that my place is at Awbrey's side," Eddy said.

"We need to get moving," Romke said. He looked up at the sun, noting its position. "We lost time with this distraction." He looked at Tucker. "Boy, you'll ride up front with me." He looked at Eddy. "We will need to talk more but not here. I won't stop you from joining us but I did warn you."

"I'll collect my horse and catch up," Eddy said.

"Indeed," Rome said, not at all pleased with the turn of events.

Tucker clambered up into the driver's bench while everyone else stepped into the wagon. Awbrey smiled and nearly bounced on her seat. It was so good to see Eddy. The wagon jerked into motion and the noisy, swaying journey continued. Awbrey smiled so much that her cheeks hurt.

"So that's your Eddy?" Sophie said as the wagon rumbled onto the road and picked up speed. "He's sort of cute in a rough sort of way. Endearing. The sort that grows on you, I suppose."

Awbrey smiled even broader. "He is endearing, yes. And handsome and kind and loyal and funny. I missed him so much!"

"I've never seen anyone in love before," Sophie said. "Ugh. You're gushy."

Awbrey just smiled. Nothing could make her feel less than totally happy now that Eddy was with the group, with her. They could still get married when they got to where they were going.

Awbrey had no idea where they were heading. Sophie would know. Sophie seemed to know everything.

"Where are we going?" Awbrey asked.

"To Garlan, of course," Sophie said.

"Garlan? But we're going in the wrong direction," Awbrey said.

"Baron Barnett would have found us immediately if we had gone east directly to Garlan. He's probably scouring every inch between Lethbridge and Garlan right now," Sophie said.

"Oakport. We're going south then? Won't he be watching Delta?" Awbrey asked, puzzled.

"We're going north again," Jaydin said, looking out the window above Awbrey's head.

"North? Back to Pindstein?" Awbrey's eyes lit up as she asked.

Jaydin shook his head. "We'll avoid Pindstein."

"Oh," Awbrey said in disappointment. The disappointment was short lived however. Eddy was with her now. Awbrey smiled as she thought about Eddy. Her Eddy had followed her.

It was dark by the time Romke stopped the wagon. They ate a cold dinner because Romke did not want a fire. Awbrey smiled every time her gaze fell on Eddy. Sophie scowled as she chewed a raw carrot, watching Awbrey and Eddy but keeping her thoughts to herself.

The girls slept inside the wagon while Romke, Eddy, Jaydin, and Tucker slept on blankets under the wagon. Gemma curled up next to Sophie on a sofa, leaving Awbrey to her own sofa.

Dawn barely lightened the sky when Romke hit the road again. Everyone in the wagon fell back asleep for several hours. When Awbrey woke from her nap Sophie was already awake but Jaydin slept on the floor between the two sofas with Tucker curled up in a ball at his feet. Gemma lay with her feet on Sophie's lap. Sophie held her embroidery hoop above Gemma's feet.

Awbrey found the book she had been reading and settled back to read. She quickly lost herself in the history of Kiel that she had never learned in school. The history was quite interesting. Details were written down that would never have made it into a school book. Though Awbrey had done well in history classes and many of the names were familiar, seen in lists and family trees, this was a history she had never heard even a hint of before. It was not a pretty picture as painted in her school history classes.

She had not known that King Osprin the Second was the bastard son of King Oin and Princess Mirandal put on the throne after a war to put him on the throne because King Osprin had gone insane. Queen Cassandril Leah had murdered her five children in their sleep then thrown herself off a cliff. That had led to the Prince Wars with Iberland.

The royals of all the neighboring countries inter-married so much that the family trees had most branches entwined. Awbrey had not yet encountered any mention of the Tiegans the book was titled after though, prompting her to absently flip through the following pages hoping to glimpse the name.

Awbrey read the afternoon away, almost forgetting that she was sitting in a wagon riding farther and farther from her life in Pindstein. It was as if the author had been there, back in ages long gone, telling the story of the royals ruling Kiel, not simply listing names, dates, and critical events. At one point she realized that the king she was reading about had lived hundreds of years earlier. So much felt the same despite the passage of time.

They had a brief, unexpected stop in late afternoon. Romke let them stretch their legs while he checked the horse's shoes but warned them not to wander out of sight. Eddy dismounted and walked next to Awbrey, guiding her away from the others. He told Awbrey that he was scouting ahead and would swing over to Pindstein when they were closer to the town.

"We're near Pindstein?" Awbrey asked, feeling a momentary surge of hope.

"Only by horseback. The wagon will stay on the west side of the Maus River," Eddy explained. He glanced around them. "Don't say anything, okay?"

"Okay. But why is it a secret?" Awbrey whispered.

"It isn't a secret. Just don't say anything. I don't want to worry anyone that I'm going into town," Eddy said.

"I want to go with you," Awbrey whispered.

Eddy shook his head. "I just want to make sure everything is all right. I have to, uh, move fast. I just wanted to let you know, just in case. Just in case I am late catching up."

"But why are you going there if it's dangerous?" Awbrey asked, sensing that he was hiding something from her.

"I left in such a hurry. I need to collect something," Eddy said.

Awbrey frowned but nodded. Eddy gave her a quick hug and mounted his horse.

Romke was definitely in a hurry after the encounter with the small band of thieves led by the angry man. As soon as he had removed the stone lodged in the horse's shoe he was ready to get moving and shuffled them back into the wagon. Romke had Tucker sit up front with him again. The wagon rattled along the road at a faster speed than Romke had used before.

"That club hanging in mid-air was pretty amazing," Jaydin said as the wagon rumbled on its way north.

Awbrey looked up from her book. Sophie looked up from playing a string game with Gemma. Gemma stared in deep concentration at the string wound around Sophie's fingers in complex web.

"I keep thinking about it. It had to be the boy or your betrothed," Jaydin said, looking at Awbrey.

"Eddy?" Awbrey asked. She laughed softly.

"I didn't feel anything," Sophie said.

"Was Eddy at Oakport?" Jaydin asked Awbrey.

"To freeze a club in mid-air, well that is amazing," Sophie said. "But I can't feel anything coming from the boy or Eddy either. If he had a talent I would feel it."

"I thought of that. You didn't say anything so I figured you didn't sense anything. Unless he's a true magician," Jaydin said.

"A true magician?" Awbrey asked, confused.

Sophie laughed. "Now that's a myth. A true magician *is* magic."

"But, but, uh, what?" Awbrey asked, wrinkling her nose.

"We have little talents of magic. A true magician can use magic any way he or she wants. Is your Eddy a magician?" Sophie asked. Awbrey shook her head, more in trying to digest the idea than denying it. "Well, someone froze that club in mid-air."

Awbrey looked back to her book but found the words on the page slippery. She read but did not know what she read. Eventually Awbrey just stared at the page, not even seeing the words. Awbrey considered the idea that Eddy had a magical talent.

If Tucker could freeze a club in mid-air surely he would have done so when his foster father was beating him. The man had not known that the boy was there. If the boy had ever done such a trick before the man would have known immediately that it was the boy. Awbrey had considered immediately that it meant Eddy must have done it. But a magician? No, not a magician. Just a talent.

That was what Eddy was trying to tell her when the thieves had shown up at the wagon and interrupted him, that he had a magical talent. That was why the apprenticeship with Jacksol would not work. As the realization hit Awbrey she looked up at Jaydin, who was staring at her thoughtfully. Jaydin shrugged but he had clearly come to the same path of thought as Awbrey. Awbrey frowned.

Magicians were a myth. Magicians were evil. Eddy was not evil. It did not matter to her if Eddy was a magician. She loved him no matter what.

"Just because you can't read or feel his talent does not mean he is a magician," Awbrey said to Sophie.

"I can always tell," Sophie said.

"Eddy is not evil," Awbrey said.

Sophie laughed harshly, dropping the thread into a tangled mess on her lap. "Why would you think he is evil just because he's a magician?"

"Not Eddy," Awbrey said.

"You are such a naïve fool. Haven't you figured out yet that magic is not evil?" Sophie asked.

"I don't think *being* magic is evil," Awbrey said. "But a magician is different. Magicians do bad things. They take over whole towns and summon demons and don't care about people."

Sophie snorted. "You believe that?"

"Summon demons?" Gemma asked, looking up from trying to untangle the string. "What are demons?"

"Nothing but imagination of the ignorant," Sophie said, glaring at Awbrey.

"I read about it," Awbrey said.

"Oh, and that makes it real?" Sophie asked.

"Everyone knows it. Everyone talks about it," Awbrey said.

"That doesn't make it right," Sophie said. "Do you believe

everything anyone tells you? No. Just the stupid, wrong stuff."

"That's enough," Jaydin said. "She just doesn't know."

"How can she have so many invalid prejudices about magic when she is magic and was raised by magic parents?" Sophie asked in frustration.

"I bet I could summon demons," Gemma said, growing thoughtful.

"No!" Sophie and Jaydin said in unison.

Awbrey wanted to cry. They were always ganging up against her. Sophie especially was always making her feel stupid. If Eddy was a magician then magicians were not evil because Eddy was not evil. Therefore Eddy could not be a magician.

It was all so confusing. Being magic did not make one a magician. Awbrey really did not know the difference even though it had felt obvious when they were talking about it. To be honest, she had thought a shape shifter was a magician, yet Jaydin did nothing but change into another form. It was all wrong.

Everything she knew was twisted and made no sense. She would have asked what it did mean then but she did not want to admit that she did not really know anything at all except for what stories she had heard from classmates growing up. Besides, Sophie always made her feel so ignorant.

Awbrey was still convinced that she was not even magic yet she was in a wagon being taken away to some unknown place because the king had declared being magic illegal. Sophie insisted that

Awbrey was magic when Awbrey knew that she was not. Awbrey felt trapped in a corner. She just wanted them to leave her alone.

Romke stopped the wagon at sunset that night and allowed a fire. Eddy was there when they stopped. Awbrey and Eddy pared and cut up potatoes until the pan Romke gave them was three quarters full. Romke shaved slices of ham off a haunch and stuffed a few pieces of ham fat down into the layers of potatoes. He stirred the ham into the potatoes, covered the pan, and set the pan in the embers at the side of the fire.

Once again Romke ordered them to stretch their legs while dinner cooked. Awbrey would have preferred some time alone with Eddy but Sophie and Jaydin walked with them. Tucker and Gemma chased fireflies nearby. Darkness fell quickly and they all returned to the campfire as night covered the area in darkness. The moon had not yet risen so the night was truly dark.

"Tomorrow we load the wagon on a ship and take the river north," Romke said.

"The river? Are we near Pindstein then?" Awbrey asked.

"We passed Pindstein early this afternoon. We are near Ava," Romke said.

For the briefest moment Awbrey had grabbed at the hope that they could return home. The idea that she could just go home and return to her normal life gave her a nice, warm, fuzzy feeling inside. Reality sank into her thoughts. If it was so simple her parents would not have sent her away with Romke to begin with. There was no going home.

"They are gone, Awbrey," Eddy whispered. "I rode into Pindstein this afternoon. Your parents are gone. The house is closed up. The business office is open but his partner is running it. He bought out your father."

"Where did they go?" Awbrey asked. It was actually a relief to learn that they had not lingered, now that she had accepted there was no going back.

Eddy shook his head. "I did not linger."

"Your family will be worried," Awbrey said.

"They are gone as well, Awbrey," Eddy said.

"Gone?" Awbrey asked.

"Gone," Eddy said.

"You did the thing with the club. Your family is magic, too?" Awbrey asked. Eddy nodded. "Is everyone magic?" she asked in surprise.

"You did something in Oakport," Jaydin said.

Eddy nodded. "I couldn't reach her in time."

"I knew it," Jaydin said.

"If so many people are magic why don't we stand up to King Eldrid and say he can't make magic illegal?" Awbrey asked.

"Not so many," Romke said, studying Eddy thoughtfully. "You are not my relative, boy. Who are you?"

"Who am I? Eddy Simpson. That is all."

"Indeed," Romke said.

Romke lifted the lid of the pan holding the ham and potatoes. Steam drifted up, filling the air with the lovely smell of food. Romke crushed a dry sprig of rosemary over the potatoes and covered the pan again. Jaydin leaned forward, breathing in the smell. Awbrey would not have been surprised if he had started drooling.

"Can I sing now?" Gemma asked.

Romke considered then nodded. Gemma hummed for a minute then opened her mouth and sang. The sound was exquisite. The words she sang made no sense to Awbrey but the song was heart-wrenching beautiful nonetheless. When Gemma finished her song she smiled and looked very pleased with herself. Nothing else happened. Nothing danced or exploded.

"How beautiful, Gemma," Awbrey said with complete sincerity.

"She did something," Sophie said, looking around. "What did you do, Gemma?"

Gemma giggled but only shook her head. "Can I sing another song?"

"Did you do something, girl?" Romke asked.

"Nothing bad," Gemma said, pouting now. "I sing good songs also. I only sing bad songs when I am angry."

"The sky," Tucker said, head bent all the way back as he stared at the sky above him.

Everyone looked up at the sky. A ribbon of green light undulated across the star speckled blackness above their heads. Bits of light danced over the green ribbon of light, forming a heart shape.

"Oh, crap," Romke said. "Is this your doing, girl?" he asked Gemma, though it could not be anything else. "Everyone can see that. I'll bet that can be seen hundreds of miles away."

"I've heard of this. To the north. Sky Fire they call it," Jaydin said.

"It's beautiful," Tucker said in awe.

"To the north, not this far south," Romke said, frowning as he stared at the display in the night sky. "And no lights forming a heart," he added, staring at Gemma.

Chapter Seven

Awbrey glanced at Eddy. He stared up at the night sky like everyone else. Eddy extended his fingers out straight and swiped his palm on his leg ever so slightly. It was a small, simple gesture, like he was brushing a piece of lint off his trousers. If Awbrey had not been looking at him she would never have seen the gesture Eddy made.

"Hey, it's gone," Tucker said. He twisted and turned, looking all over the sky but it was now just a normal black sky dotted with stars.

"Hopefully no one noticed it. Ah, who am I kidding? Lots of people saw it. But they can't know that it originated here," Romke said.

"Where did it go?" Gemma asked. Gemma frowned as she studied the sky. A hint of anger flared in her eyes. "It should have lasted all night." Gemma looked around the people sitting with her around the campfire. "Someone broke it."

"We're lucky it was brief. I don't know how far it was seen but we don't need that kind of attention," Romke said.

"If it was seen far away then just about anyone could have…well, whatever they did to it," Awbrey said, careful to avoid looking at Eddy.

"Did you move the stars?" Tucker asked, still looking up, hoping to see the green ribbon dancing across the sky with sparkles of light forming a heart over the ribbon.

"No. Just the light," Gemma said.

Romke studied Eddy thoughtfully. Awbrey decided the potatoes needed checking and used a stick to push the lid off the pan. The smell of food released with the steam distracted the hungry travelers. Gradually the topic of the brief display of green light dancing in the sky was dropped. The potatoes were done and Sophie used a large serving spoon to dish up plates full of the food. Jaydin took a bite that was far too hot and huffed with his mouth open. Steam poured out of his mouth and he swallowed then took another too hot bite.

"I just don't understand why we have to run away," Awbrey said, setting down her empty plate. She looked around the campfire at the people Romke had collected. "If no one uses their magic and just lives a normal life, no one breaks the new law."

"What is a normal life? For me it is normal to be myself. Being myself means stretching my muscles into other shapes," Jaydin said.

"I could never sing?" Gemma asked. "I have to sing."

"How do I ignore the animals? It would be like trying to ignore thunder during a storm," Sophie said. "It's just there. Feeling other's magic is like feeling a breeze. How do you stop that, Awbrey?"

"Uh, I suppose," Awbrey said slowly. She sat up straighter. "They why can't you just stand up to the Baron and tell him that he can't make it illegal to be yourself?"

"You seem to think you aren't involved in this. You. You. Yourself. It's us, Awbrey," Sophie muttered.

"Indeed," Romke said. "You are young, child. It is not so simple."

"It should be," Awbrey said, ignoring Sophie.

Romke chuckled then shook his head. "Stand up. That is war. You need an army to do that. A handful of children does not make an army." Romke waved his arm around the campfire. "Even if all the magic folk in the country banded together it would be a pitiful little army." Romke leaned closer to Awbrey. "Could you kill someone, child?"

Kill someone? Awbrey pulled back in horror at the idea of killing a person. "No," she said.

"I could," Gemma said.

"Indeed." Romke turned his head to look at the feisty girl. "I am learning that you are a blood-thirsty one," Romke said to Gemma. He straightened. "But most magic folk are like our little Awbrey here, horrified at the idea of taking a life."

"Most people were already uncomfortable around magic folk," Eddy said. "When this new law is announced it will give them freedom to hunt out anyone different and destroy them."

Romke nodded. "The man has the way of it."

"It isn't right," Awbrey insisted. "It makes as much sense as making it illegal to have red hair."

Eddy took Awbrey's hand and raised it to his mouth. He kissed the back of her hand. "Your need for fairness is one of the things I love about you, Awbrey. One day you will have to see the reality and not the dream."

Awbrey jerked her hand out of Eddy's grasp. For some reason that she could not explain, his statement irritated her. It made no sense to her that someone could announce that it was illegal to be yourself. Every inch of her body protested at the unfairness of the whole thing. Awbrey wanted to scream in frustration.

"It is not reality to treat people like criminals when they have not done anything wrong," Awbrey said. Sophie's eyes narrowed as she stared at Awbrey.

"I'm talking about the reality that life is not fair," Eddy said. "You are all that is fair and good so you don't see that some people don't see life that way."

Sophie snorted. Awbrey ignored Sophie, letting the words sink in. Some of the irritation left her but not all. "The king should be fair and good. It's up to him to take care of the kingdom."

This time Sophie laughed. "Eldrid is king because his father was king. He is weak, insecure, and an arrogant ass."

"He is still our king," Awbrey said. "You shouldn't say such things."

"You only say that because you haven't met him. Besides, you throw your little tantrums about fairness and letting people live their lives and you are as shallow as any of them. You keep denying your magic and acting like you are apart from us, better than us magic folk. The thought of your Eddy being a magician was enough to send you into a panic because magicians are evil. If you can't have an open mind how can you expect anyone else to?" Sophie said, voice rising with each word until she was yelling.

"Let it be," Romke said.

Sophie stood "I need to visit the trees. You may as well come with, Gemma."

"I'll guard you," Tucker said, jumping to his feet.

"You'll peek," Gemma said.

"No, I won't. Promise," Tucker said.

"I'd better make sure he doesn't," Jaydin said. He stood and stretched before slowly following the others.

"I never said you were evil," Awbrey said to Eddy.

"I know," Eddy said.

"She just doesn't like me," Awbrey said. "I am not saying anything is wrong with being magic. I am defending magic people. I am just not magic. Why won't anyone believe me?"

"You are not the only one torn from all that she loves, being threatened," Romke said.

Awbrey opened her mouth to protest then shut it without saying anything. Sophie had started out nice enough, she realized. It was as the days passed that Sophie had gotten angry and impatient with Awbrey. Thinking about what Romke said, Awbrey realized that she had been slightly self-absorbed and might even have said a few things that could be taken the wrong way.

Awbrey was a smart girl with a good head on her shoulders. She was willing to concede that perhaps she had not behaved as well as she maybe could have. Awbrey grimaced as she remembered her pouting and feeling that she was different than the rest and had no business being with them. It was just that she was different because she was not magic.

"What do you plan on doing with the boy?" Eddy asked Romke. Eddy took Awbrey's hand and rubbed the back of her hand with his thumb soothingly.

Romke shrugged. "For now he must stay with us." Romke stirred up the fire with a stick and tossed more wood onto the flames. "We can't risk his telling tales of traveling in a wagon with a man who turns into a wolf and a girl who makes the stars dance. I'll find a good home for him when the time is right."

"Is everyone related to you truly magic?" Awbrey asked. Romke nodded. "Then perhaps I just don't know what my magic is," Awbrey said.

Romke smiled. "It is the first step."

"First step?" Awbrey asked.

"Being willing to concede that there is the actual possibility that your parents did not send you off on this adventure for no reason. If you were not magic I would not have brought you with, Awbrey. If you want to get along with the other girl you will need to stop distancing yourself from us. You are part of this magical family."

"If everyone related to you is magic then you must be magic. What is your magic?" Awbrey asked.

"A shield. The lack of magic. No magic gets through to me," Romke said.

"I don't understand," Awbrey said.

"If our little singer wanted to make me dance a jig it wouldn't work on me. Your mother's little whispers would not work on me. My brother could turn anyone into an animal of his choice. It didn't work on me. Fortunately I have never experienced snuffling in the mud as a pig," Rome said, smiling at a distant memory.

Romke looked across the fire at Eddy. "Again. Who are you?"

"My parents came from across the sea when I was a young child," Eddy said. "I don't remember much before that long voyage. We settled in Pindstein. That's all there is to tell."

"Your family? They have the same abilities as you?"

Eddy shook his head. "Only my father. He has been teaching me since it displayed itself. We suspect Sonata might have some talent. Maybe another year and it will display with her. Or not."

"Displayed?" Romke looked puzzled by the word. "That is new. Displayed, huh?"

Eddy chuckled. "I apologize. I'm so used to the term that I didn't realize it was, uh, specific," he said. "I mean, uh, make itself known? The magic comes out as a person matures. Much like body parts sprouting of a certain age. Much like one notices hair growing where it had not grown before, suddenly you see things a little differently, feel things a little differently."

"You use spells?" Romke asked.

Eddy shook his head. "No. It's more of seeing how things are made and manipulating their natural state to suit me. Like the club. I made the air around it solid."

"The lights in the sky?" Romke asked.

"I released the artificial boundaries holding it in place and it reverted to normal," Eddy said.

"Try it on me," Romke said.

"What?"

"Try your magic on me," Romke said.

Eddy considered the request then gave several minutes thought before smiling as an idea hit him. Romke waited. Awbrey watched them. Nothing happened. Eddy tilted his head thoughtfully, studying Romke.

"You said shield and that's a good description," Eddy said.

"You tried then?" Romke asked. "No gestures. No words. No nothing. I didn't feel anything. You really tried on me? Directly on me?"

Awbrey attention drifted and she only half listened to the two men continue to talk of magic. She looked up at the dark sky with its speckling of stars. Someone a hundred miles away would be seeing the same sky. Someone had undoubtedly seen Gemma's little light trick. Could they see the same view of the sky as far away as Lethbridge?

Maybe there was something wrong with her, Awbrey wondered. There was just something about thinking about people being magic that made her skin crawl. Knowing Jaydin, Sophie, and Gemma it did not bother her that they were magic. It was when she thought of the idea of magic, of unknown people using magic that she felt uncomfortable. Awbrey could not control the feelings of discomfort.

"I have shared some basic things with you as I respect you and understand that you are aiding Awbrey," Eddy said. "But don't expect me to bare all."

"It's just different," Romke said. "I think you are what they call a natural magician." Something in Eddy's facial expression at hearing the term made Romke sit up straighter. "Ah. When I was a younger man I traveled around the world. In a land far away I was arrested for performing magic when a spoiled local bully, son of a high ranking lord, tried to use a magic trick on me. It failed, of course. The lord had me arrested. He brought in a local magician, who promptly told Lord So-and-So that I was not magic. Now that I am reminded of the ordeal, you bear a startling resemblance to that man."

Eddy laughed at the idea. "The Lord or the magician?"

"Both. The two were brothers."

"You have a startling memory for faces. How many years ago did you briefly know that man?" Eddy said.

"I remember," Romke insisted.

Eddy shrugged. "I do not know if I have an ancestor from your mysterious land. My parents refused to talk of where we came from or our life in that land. If it wasn't for that horrendous trip across the sea I doubt I would even remember that I was not born and raised in Kiel."

"Hmph," Romke said, sinking into his memories for several minutes.

Awbrey yawned. She covered her mouth with her hand and gave herself a little shake. It sounded to her like Eddy was not a magician at all. He simply had a talent like everyone else along on Romke's journey. She rested her head on Eddy's arm and stared into the dancing fire.

"You have something in the wagon," Eddy said. "Something that pulls in magic and holds it."

Romke jerked out of his reverie. He didn't say anything for a long time. "Indeed," he said at last. "That's better not mentioned."

Awbrey perked up. "In the secret compartment under the sofa? Is that's what's in the secret compartment?" Awbrey asked in interest. "Jaydin wouldn't let me look," Awbrey added when Romke glared at her.

"I can hide it for you," Eddy said. "But I need to know what it is and why you have it."

"Can't you tell?" Romke asked.

Eddy shook his head. "I just feel it pulling in magic. I can stop it from leeching the magic as well."

"I stole it from Baron Barnett," Rome said. "He used to see

the future."

"A crystal ball," Eddy said, frowning. Romke nodded. Eddy raised his eyebrows in surprise then turned his head and looked at the wagon. "There. Now no one with magic will sense it and it will stop leeching the magic."

Awbrey opened her mouth then closed it without saying anything. Romke had stolen a magical object from the baron who used it to see the future. The same baron who was responsible for making magic illegal owned a crystal ball. The same baron who made magic illegal because it was evil to alter destiny was using a crystal ball to read the future.

"Do you need to be magic to use it?" Awbrey asked, sitting up straight.

"Now don't go thinking I will let you use that thing. It is an abomination," Romke said.

"But do you have to be magic to use it?" Awbrey persisted.

"Yes," Eddy said. "It holds the magic because it takes so much to use but you would have to be magic to release the magic and see what you want to see."

"Then Baron Barnett must be magic," Awbrey said. Both men stared at her as the implication set in. "I'll bet he can't see you in it either, Uncle Romke. That's why he was able to find all the magic users in Lethbridge but you managed to get out with Sophie and Jaydin."

"Indeed," Romke said thoughtfully. "Indeed." He stared at

Awbrey. "There's a brain in that sulky head after all. But he could have had someone who is magic use it for him. Just because he has it doesn't mean he used it himself. But I do want to ponder on the idea that I don't show up in his crystal ball."

Awbrey stiffened. Sulky? She was not sulky. How would Romke like being yanked out of his comfortable life for no reason, tossed into a stifling, uncomfortable wagon day after day, trapped in that wagon with the irritating, condescending Sophie and then be referred to as sulky?

"He must be magic," Awbrey said.

Romke shook his head. "No, child. Having the crystal ball does not mean he is magic. Besides, Sophie would have said something if he is magic."

"Walk with me before we turn in for the night," Eddy said to Awbrey, pulling her to her feet.

They walked along the dirt path leading back to the road, the lighter gravel visible under the light from the rising moon. Awbrey glanced over her shoulder at Romke. The man was sitting there staring into the fire, deep in his thoughts. Movement caught her eye and she looked beyond Romke. Sophie's light colored gown was visible beyond the camp area as the small group wandered back to the campfire.

"I am not sulky," Awbrey said. She sighed. "I don't mean to be anyway."

"I know," Eddy said, taking her hand.

They spoke of light topics as they slowly picked their way in the darkness. Getting away from the fire's light helped their eyes adjust to the darkness and it became easier to see the outline of the path as they walked. They avoided speaking of magic or their mad dash across the country to outrun news of a law that would instantly make them criminals.

As Awbrey listened to Eddy talk about the antics of Abigail's little dog the night before the planned betrothal dinner Awbrey relaxed. She chuckled, clearly picturing the little dog steal a whole tray of Cook's infamous bacon tarts minutes before they were to be served. A sense of normalcy settled over her for a few minutes. Awbrey chuckled louder as she listed to Eddy tell of Cook chasing the dog through the house, the dog constantly circling back to the fallen tray to snatch another treat. They reached the road and stopped and turned back.

As they turned to walk back to the camp area Awbrey saw the wagon silhouetted in front of the fire. Vague figures and shadows moved about the campfire. Gemma with her childish personality and a magical talent requiring great maturity to control it sat next to the fire poking at the flames with a stick.

Sophie, so fail and exactly what Awbrey always imagined a princess to be, was scrubbing the pan used to make the evening meal. Her almost white blonde hair gleamed in the firelight. If she was a princess she certainly did not shirk on normal tasks needing to be done.

Romke, a tower of strength, responsibility, and ability was checking on the horses. Little Tucker trailed him like a shadow. Romke reached down and scooped Tucker up and onto the back of a horse before leading the animal to a fresh grazing spot. Tucker slipped and slid on the horse's back even though the horse was casually walking at a sedate pace next to Romke.

Jaydin was cleaning the plates and utensils, wiping each plate with his finger to get every scrap of food before placing the dish into a bucket of soapy water. He spilled a generous amount of water out of the bucket as he scrubbed the plate clean then plunged it into a bucket of clean water and rubbed a towel across the plate to finish the process. Jaydin was as patient with Awbrey as Sophie was impatient with Awbrey.

"I don't belong with them," Awbrey said, stopping. "I have no magic."

"You wouldn't be here if your parents did not feel you would be in danger if you stayed," Eddy said. "Do you really think they would have sent you out with Romke other than because they felt it was the safest thing for you? Besides, I belong here, with them, and you belong at my side."

Awbrey stepped into Eddy's arms and rested her head on his chest. Eddy had a way of saying just the right thing. He was right. He belonged with these people and where he was that was where Awbrey wanted to be. Awbrey just wished that Eddy wanted it to be back at Pindstein.

"We could leave now. Go home. No one would ever know you are magic. I never knew," Awbrey said.

"No," Eddy said. "You are the one in danger if we did that. This is where you belong."

"Me? How can I be in more danger than you?" Awbrey asked in surprise.

"I just feel that you need to be here, with them," Eddy said, frowning at some thought. He shook his head. "I can't explain it."

"Sophie can talk to animals. Jaydin can turn into animals. Gemma can move the stars with a song. I don't do anything," Awbrey said. "I would feel like a fraud if I had ever said I was magic. Sophie thinks I am trying to distance myself. It isn't that at all. I think what they do is amazing. I'm a fake. Except I never said I could do magic."

"I had a dream the other night," Eddy said. "In that dream I soared in the stars like an eagle. I saw a pool of water and dived. While under water there were tunnels and I couldn't find my way out but I didn't drown either."

"That's a house cleaning dream," Awbrey said without hesitation.

"House cleaning?" Eddy asked.

She could feel his steady heartbeat under her ear. "It means nothing. Just your mind sorting the day's thoughts."

"Last night I had a dream that I was riding past a house. The house had burnt halfway down. A man was standing inside the black, charred remains and gestured for me to come in. It was Master Carlins. I entered the burnt house and he led me up the stairs. It wasn't burnt down upstairs. It seemed odd that upstairs it wasn't burnt though while downstairs everything was gone but some half walls. There was a balcony off the main bedroom but it was dark and I couldn't see anything."

Awbrey gasped. "Poor Master Carlins. I remember him. Either his wife has died or soon will. A violent death."

"The first dream I made up," Eddy said. "The second dream was real."

Awbrey pulled her head back and looked up at Eddy's face. "Why would you tell me a made up dream?"

"To prove to you that you always know," Eddy said. "You knew right away that it meant nothing and it didn't. Embrace your talent, Awbrey."

"I didn't really think of it as a talent," Awbrey said, resting her head on his chest again.

"Every morning learn the others' dreams of the night. Use it," Eddy said. "Learn more. There's always more to learn."

"Learn it? But I don't want to embrace it. I don't want to be magic. I just want to live a normal life. The life I had."

"Why?" Eddy asked. "Why do you fight it so hard?"

Awbrey considered. "I don't know. I guess I just don't feel that it's real."

Eddy groaned in frustration. "You keep going back and forth.

Just try, Awbrey."

"All right," Awbrey said slowly. She did not feel that it would do any good but she would try. For Eddy.

"Time to turn in," Romke yelled out in their direction.

Awbrey did not know if Romke could see them standing out there but when Eddy lowered his head to steal a good night kiss she danced out of his arms without more than a quick peck on the lips. She had no intention of an audience watching her and Eddy kissing.

Eddy pretended to growl. "I thought you liked my kisses."

"It's an audience I don't like," Awbrey said. She smiled in the dark and reached up on her tiptoes to kiss Eddy's lips in a quick, chaste kiss, then darted back to the wagon.

The next morning Awbrey thought about what Eddy had said regarding honing her dream talent as they started out again. The wagon swayed and rumbled onto the road and picked up speed. The sky visible through the windows was a blend of gray and teal, a deep rich teal. The same teal that bordered a peacock's tail feather.

She had seen one once, a peacock feather. Her father had brought it home to show her mother. A sailor had given the feather to him. Her mother had smiled as she held the feather but it was a sad smile and her father had taken it back to the sailor the next day. Awbrey had not known why the sight of a peacock feather made her mother so sad. She might never know. Awbrey missed her mother, both her parents, so much at that moment, looking out at the teal sky.

Jaydin sat at an angle in the corner of the same sofa Awbrey sat on, eyes closed. She could feel that he was still awake though. Sophie had placed the lantern near her and was reading a book, telling Gemma tidbits as she read. Gemma was not interested in what Sophie was reading and was trying to play a string game by herself. Tucker was lying on the floorboards sleeping. The boy lay flat on his back with his limbs sprawled and mouth hanging open.

Awbrey licked her lips. All she had to do was ask their dreams of the night yet the words stuck in her throat. Awbrey cleared her throat. Eddy thought it was a good idea. Awbrey cleared her throat again, trying to work up the courage to ask them to share their dreams with her.

Sophie looked up over her book. "Do you have a frog in your throat?" she asked Awbrey.

Gemma giggled. "Frog."

"I was just wondering, you see. I was just thinking. Did you dream last night?" Awbrey asked.

"I did," Gemma said, dropping the string. "I had a dream that I made the lights dance and a big hand erased the lights. So I made the flowers dance and the hand made them stop."

"Interesting," Awbrey said. "Sophie?"

Sophie studied Awbrey thoughtfully. She lowered the book to her lap. "I did. I dreamt that a white snake was moving to a nest of duck eggs. The mother duck tried to lure away the snake but the snake ignored her and kept moving to the eggs. The eggs started hatching. The snake snatched an egg that was cracked but the baby duck never emerged. An owl swooped down and grabbed the snake and flew away."

"How sad," Awbrey said. Awbrey looked over at Jaydin. His eyes were open now. "Jaydin?"

"Aren't you going to say what they mean?" Jaydin asked.

"Not yet," Awbrey said.

"The hand made the flowers stop so I found a batch of nettles and slapped the hand with the nettles," Gemma said.

"Of course you did," Awbrey said in a patient voice. "Jaydin?"

Jaydin sighed and sat up straight. He rubbed his neck. "I dreamt that I was a wolf running in a pack. We were hunting. Though I was hungry I was more interested in a she-wolf running beside me," Jaydin said, neck flushing red. "She had the most lovely mane."

"I see," Awbrey said.

"Well? What do they mean?" Sophie asked.

"I made the nettles burn when I hit the hand," Gemma said.

"I have to think about it," Awbrey said, glancing at Sophie. The frail blonde was not going to like what her dream meant.

"No you don't," Jaydin said. "What don't you want us to know?"

"Gemma is just making things up," Awbrey said. "Jaydin, you are not sure if you a person who changes into a wolf or a wolf who turns into a person. You are realizing that you might be both, which is why another wolf could be a potential mate." Awbrey looked at Sophie. Her stomach tightened but she plunged into the reading anyway. "Sophie, you are the white snake and the owl is the baron."

Sophie frowned. "I would not eat baby ducks."

"Dreams are symbols. Sometimes the brain uses drastic symbols to get your attention. The snake was just being a snake. The owl is the baron's sigil, right? And he snatched you while you were being true to your nature."

"That's nonsense. What does that have to do with the future?" Sophie asked.

"I don't know that it does. Very few dreams are about the future. Unless, maybe he catches you because you are being you. But I don't think it's about the future. I think it's about you fearing Baron Barnett."

"Do you interpret your own dreams?" Jaydin asked.

Awbrey nodded. They seemed angry with her about the meaning of their dreams. "Why are you so upset?" she asked Sophie. "It is your dream. You dreamed it."

"I see myself as the mother duck. Not a white snake going after ducklings. It's cruel of you to say I am the white snake," Sophie said.

"Yet you refrain from using your magic. You must be afraid that it will bring the baron down on you."

"What makes you think I haven't used it?" Sophie asked.

"Why, I've never seen you do anything," Awbrey said.

"There is nothing to see," Sophie said. "Why do you think Black Star, Fall Moon, and Running Water remained calm when a bear showed up? I convinced them that they were safe. And that man's horse was ready to run nonstop to the ocean to get away from the bear. If he had left that angry man would have had no way to retreat. I told him that he had to stay."

Sophie held her book up, blocking her face in the only way available to make a dramatic exit. Within seconds she lowered the book again. "Every day I visit with the horses, birds, and squirrels. I cannot stop being me just because some old man with a red nose and caterpillar eyebrow convinced Eldrid that magic is evil."

"You can hide it though," Jaydin said. "No one would ever know that you are magic. I can't hide."

The shutter at the front of the wagon slid open. "We are almost to the dock. Hold off on the bickering back there," Romke said through the opening.

Chapter Eight

The group instantly silenced. Romke looked around the wagon. Satisfied that they could restrain themselves from continuing the argument, he slid the shutter shut. There was some glaring going on but no one spoke. The silence disrupted Tucker's sleep and he sat up, rubbing the sleep from his eyes. The boy looked around, sensing the build-up of frustrated anger filling the wagon.

Just as Romke said, the wagon soon pulled to a stop and the back door opened a minute later. Eddy stuck his head in the door. Behind him the river stretched out like a wide blue ribbon with the sun's reflections dancing in the ripples. Eddy looked around the wagon at the angry faces. "C'mon. They need to load the wagon," he said.

Tucker escaped before Eddy even finished talking, ducking under Eddy's arm that he was using to hold the door open. Jaydin was quick to follow. Awbrey went behind Jaydin. Eddy took her hand and helped her down the two steps. Romke was unharnessing the horses. Sophie and Gemma followed at Awbrey's heels. Several burly men surrounded the wagon. Eddy shut and latched the door then nodded at the burly men.

The small group gathered out of the way, together but apart. Awbrey grabbed Tucker's hand and held him in a firm grip to keep him out of the way as the men worked. The last thing they needed was the boy to be crushed under the wagon or knocked into the river. The boy tugged futilely for a few minutes, eager to move closer to the action, then gradually watched the loading with his complete attention.

A handful of seagulls hung around the dock, occasionally filling the air with their distinct cries. A dog wandered up to the group, pacing restlessly for a few minutes and whining. A seagull flew at the dog's head then landed next to the dog, tilting its head as it approached the animal. Sophie crouched down and the dog immediately ran up to her, wiggling its rear end and leaning against her leg, almost knocking the girl off her feet.

As soon as the horses were freed from the hitch the men put their strong hands on the wagon sides and pushed it the remaining distance to the dock. At the side of the dock in the water was a large, flat-bottomed ship. Romke led the horses one at a time up thick, wide planks leaning between the ship and dock to a small fenced area in the center of the ship. Eddy led his horse up one of the planks onto the ship as well.

"We are going on that boat?" Tucker asked, eyes wide.

"It's a ship," Jaydin said.

"I've never been on a boat," Tucker said.

"It's a ship," Jaydin said.

"I've never been on a ship or boat," Tucker said. He pressed his small body against Awbrey's leg. "Not sure I want to be on a ship or boat."

"It will be fine," Awbrey said. My father and brother are on ships and boats all the time."

Stacked hay bales formed a wall around three sides of the fence, almost hiding that there was a fence there. A thick layer of straw had been spread out to cover the decking within the fenced area. The area within the fence was not even large enough to allow the horses to move around. Each one was securely tied to the fence rail. Moving horses on a ship disrupted the center of balance. All four horses immediately began eating the hay through the fencing.

The men pushed the wagon to the planks, backing up and testing the position a few times, then running the wagon up the planks and onto the deck. They pushed it into place next to the fence, securing it by the horses. Eddy returned to Awbrey's side after his horse was secured. Awbrey walked up the plank next to Eddy. The efficient men were securing the wagon wheels to braces in the deck with wrist-thick ropes. Then they ran straps over the axles as well. Even during a thunderstorm that wagon was not going to shift an inch on the ship.

Eddy whistled as he watched them work. "They are really good. I have never seen a wagon loaded so efficiently. That only took them minutes from shore side to being on deck and secured."

"They make it look easy," Awbrey said in agreement."

"I should see if…oh, right. Never mind," Eddy said, frowning. "It's easy to forget. I thought… well, it doesn't matter."

Awbrey had never seen Eddy so unsettled. "What, Eddy?"

Eddy laughed. "I just thought it would be nice to hire away these men. But there's no place to hire them to, right? No more shipping business."

Awbrey watched the burly men working. She knew what Eddy was talking about. Her father would love to employ such workers for his ships. Eddy was thinking the same for his family's business, forgetting for a moment the circumstances that had changed their lives. The Simpsons were gone from Pindstein now as well.

Awbrey looked around them as they waited. Two buildings sat up on shore a little way from the river bank. The buildings and dock were the only structures in sight. More trees stretched out into the distance to the northeast. To the southeast were rolling hills with scrub terrain, bushes and small clumps of trees. To the north a bend in the river blocked the view. Across the river a thin line of trees bordered the bank but beyond that was a flat plain of grasses with nothing else in sight.

"Is this Ava?" Awbrey asked. She scrunched her face, trying to remember. It seemed that she had been to Ava with her father when she was a child but she remembered a lovely town. Certainly more than two buildings.

"We're a few miles south of Ava," Romke said. "This dock is a private dock. Ava is around the bend in the river."

Romke gestured for everyone to board the ship. Sophie patted the dog's head and stood straight. The dog whined when Sophie took a few steps to the ship. Sophie ignored the dog and it trotted up the bank and sat watching them. Once everyone was aboard and the ship's men had everything secured in the proper place the captain approached Romke. They stepped aside and had a brief discussion. Romke handed a small coin purse to the captain. The captain tossed the bag in the air and caught it in his palm. He nodded and turned away.

The exchange of money was the cue to remove the heavy ropes from the dock posts and use poles to push the ship free of the dock's security. Though there was a mast and heavy canvas sails hanging from the mast none of the burly men touched the sails. The captain let the current pull them out into the river.

"I did say we are in a hurry," Romke said to the captain.

"Sail has to wait. We pass the town first," the captain said.

Eddy nodded as he listened, looking up at the approaching bend. "There's a large pier at Ava. A lot of boats in the water. I remember now," Eddy said to Awbrey. "No sails allowed in the area. A ship this size would demolish a little fishing boat."

Awbrey saw the smoke first as they rounded the bend. Small lines of gray smoke drifted into the air and dissipated quickly. Then she saw the charred remains of several houses on the southern edge of town. Sophie and Gemma crowded up against the ship's guard rail near Awbrey. More burnt buildings were becoming visible. More smoke idly rose deeper within the town, thin lines rising straight up.

"What happened here?" Romke asked the captain.

"King's men rode into town with an edict. Any magic user was to be declared a treasonous outlaw and anyone aiding such a criminal was to share his or her fate," the captain said.

"There are that many magic users here?" Awbrey asked in surprise. There were at least twenty or thirty houses burnt or burning visible along the riverbank and many more in the interior of the town.

"Nah," the captain said. He turned his head and spit over the guard rail. "Fools. I doubt there was even one. There was a frenzy and a house was fired. Started neighboring buildings on fire. A few more got fired in the frenzy."

Seven pairs of eyes intently watched the town slide past while the captain and his men eased the ship farther from shore. Some buildings stood whole with scorch marks around windows and doors. Next to them half a building was all that remained after the fire. There was nearly a half mile stretch where nothing but black rubble remained. Behind the empty half mile stretch more burnt buildings could be seen, forming a crooked line into the town center.

They approached the main city dock, a cluster of piers reaching out into the river, the reason the captain was working so hard at putting distance between the bank and his ship. Two ships were moored at the pier, both gutted by fire. Thick ropes held the partially submerged burnt remains securely to the dock. The wind now brought the smell across the river. It was a horrible smell, more than wood had burned in those fires. Many things had burned.

They could clearly see the people standing on the piers. Some townspeople watched the ship go past, faces turned to the river, staring intently at the ship carrying its passengers past the ravaged town. They were also visible to the people on the piers, standing along the rail, staring in shock. Some people only glanced their way but did not care about the ship sailing past, focus on their immediate situation. What the people on the pier were thinking as they stood watching the ship pass their burnt town was hard to know.

Awbrey clutched Eddy's hand. So much destruction. Such pointless, mindless destruction. Businesses and homes were gone, wiped away by one rash act of someone acting in fear. It slowly dawned on Awbrey that it was likely more than buildings and their contents destroyed by the fire.

"Were many people hurt?" Sophie asked.

"I'm sure," the captain said. "We stayed with the ship. Guarded her. Luckily we were at the south dock. Not as much commotion there."

"Hear of any similar towns?" Romke asked.

The captain shook his head. "Don't know. No ships coming down stopped once they saw the mess. The news went north at the same time. Lots of gossip about that during the day before Ava burned."

"Hopefully it was an isolated event," Romke said, gaze locked on the pier. "I am glad you stayed."

"I owe Hans Tieg. Besides, this is his ship until I deliver you. That's the deal. If I don't deliver you I don't get the ship," the captain said. "She's a nice ship. Worth the price."

Awbrey looked at the captain in surprise. He knew her father. These burly men likely already worked for her father. This was her father's ship. Awbrey did not need Eddy's gentle squeeze on her hand to warn her to stay silent. The burning town on the river's shore stole all her words and most of her thoughts.

"Raise the sail," the captain yelled.

With a loud thump and crackling whoosh, the sail rose and caught the wind. The sailors moved about gracefully, using ropes to set the sail. The sail gave one more crack then the ship lurched forward. Everyone looked up at the sail with mixed reactions.

"It's such a bright blue," Eddy said in surprise, head tilted back as he stared at the sail.

"Aye," the captain said with a grin. "Makes a statement."

"I'm not sure we want to make such a statement," Romke said.

"Men see statements. Today they see a bright blue sail. Tomorrow, after the sun has reacted with the solution the canvas was soaked in, a yellow sail. While anyone seeing us sail away under a bright blue sail and go looking. Those men won't give a yellow sail a second look."

"What did he say?" Awbrey asked Eddy.

"That the sail will change from blue to yellow after a day in the sun. Anyone seeing us pass today with a blue sail will not look twice at a ship with a yellow sail," Eddy explained.

"Perhaps," Romke said. "They might have noticed the wagon instead of the sail."

"Tomorrow they won't see a wagon," the captain said. "But everyone will see the blue sail. Ain't no missing that blue sail."

"I tend to agree," Eddy said to Awbrey. "That is one *blue* sail."

The journey up the river went smoothly. The current was strong, the wind filled the sails, and the shore flew past. The Maus River flowed generally westerly down out of the mountains to Pindstein where it then veered south after meeting the North River. The North River flowed north. Where the two rivers met the currents churned or did not move at all, which was why Romke had chosen to take the river near Ava instead of at Pindstein. The route between Pindstein and Ava was sailable but prone to delays and complications that he had no time for.

The first noticeable benefit of riding the river was that on a clear night with a moon in the sky an experienced captain could travel all night as well. When they woke the wagon had vanished from sight. In its place was a stack of crates and barrels. Awbrey rubbed her eyes and looked again. Now she could see that the crates were painted on a tarp and hung perfectly to cover the wagon with a few real crates to supplement the effect. The sail was a butter yellow with a few faded blue streaks at the bottom.

The crew had hung a curtain for the girls to provide privacy from all the men on the ship. The ship's rail was solid wood, polished until it shined. Gemma had a difficult time using a bucket to relieve her bladder. Sophie told the girl she could sing a song if she peed in the bucket. Gemma was so excited that she used the bucket right away. Awbrey rolled up the mats while Sophie rolled up the blankets.

Awbrey eyed the bucket dubiously but took her turn. Squatting over a bucket with a thin blanket between her and the men and an open shoreline on a rolling deck did not make it easy to relax enough to relieve her bladder, however, even if the guard rail was high enough to block anyone's view from shore, if there was someone on shore. Awbrey closed her eyes, pictured herself somewhere else, anywhere else. Eventually nature won and the need was greater than the distractions around her.

Gemma peered over the side of the ship. She had to stand on her tiptoes to see over the rail because it sloped. A soft hum filled the air before Gemma began to sing. Water rose in spirals. Fish jumped through water rings.

"How fun," Awbrey said, standing next to Gemma and watching the river come to life. "Are the fish dancing?"

Gemma smiled and nodded. She only sang for a few minutes. When she stopped singing the river settled back to normal. Sophie stood on Gemma's other side, studying the river thoughtfully while she tapped her chin with her finger. Gemma stared out at the water for several minutes.

"My heart is heavy today. The song helped. But not enough," Gemma said.

"Gemma," Sophie said. "Do you think you could bring a spiral of water up onto the ship? Like a waterfall? And maybe warm it a bit as well?"

Gemma shrugged. "Sure."

Sophie's face lit up. "I will grab the soap. And I suppose warn someone so they don't come running to see if the ship is flooding. I am going to have a shower!"

When Sophie warned the men in their group they wanted to share the opportunity to clean so Gemma held a long line of water as everyone took a turn stepping behind the curtain under her warm waterfall. Gemma swept the soapy used water right back over the rail. By the time Sophie and Awbrey had bathed the girl was growing tired so the men and Tucker stepped behind the curtain together. Once the men were done, Gemma even brought the waterfall over her own head to clean herself. Being clean cheered everyone and the mood of the group that had been growing darker lightened considerably.

"I wish I had a clean dress to put on," Awbrey said as they sat cross-legged on the deck combing out their hair. "I wasn't really thinking clearly when I packed. The two dresses I brought with would not be appropriate for sitting on a ship deck." Awbrey turned Gemma so that the girl's back was to her and began working on her hair. "Thank you so much, Gemma. It feels wonderful to be clean."

"You are most wonderfully welcome," Gemma said. The girl yawned and covered her mouth. "I should have eaten breakfast first. I am tired and I'm as hungry as Jaydin."

"Did you learn anything, Sophie?" Awbrey asked as she combed Gemma's snarls out of her hair.

"What do you mean?" Sophie asked, freezing with her comb in her hair.

"If I could speak to animals I would have asked any I could find what happened," Awbrey said. "Surely some cat or dog or horse saw things." Awbrey paused in her task. "Some stray dog wandering about the dock?"

Sophie nodded and resumed combing her hair. She combed for a few minutes then put her comb away. "It isn't so simple but I have me a good idea. The mob came to a house. The mob was led by a man wearing an owl on his chest."

"An owl? But Eldrid's sigil is a rearing stallion," Awbrey said. She divided Gemma's hair and began braiding.

"Indeed," Romke said, approaching with breakfast. He set down a basket with hard biscuits and dried fish. "The owl is the baron's sigil."

"The baron? Why would one of the baron's men be leading?" Awbrey asked.

"Indeed," Romke said. "Continue, girl."

Sophie nodded. "They dragged a woman and a boy out of the house. The man with the owl on his chest talked to the woman for a few minutes then the man entered the house while the mob held the woman. When the man came out of the house flames came out of the windows." Sophie paused, taking a deep breath.

Gemma picked up a second biscuit and took a bite. Awbrey forgot about braiding hair. She stared at Sophie with her complete attention. The rest had wandered up to them and listened quietly.

"The flames jumped to nearby houses. No one was fighting fire. They were too busy being a mob," Sophie said. She turned her head and stared off into the distance. Sophie took another deep breath and continued, still staring off into the distance. "At the third house the woman who lived there yelled at the mob through an upstairs window. They went into the house and dragged her out with her two children. They hung the children."

Sophie was unable to continue. Awbrey stared at the frail, blonde girl in shock. Sophie was crying. She sobbed and gasped for breath. Gemma got to her knees and moved closer to Sophie. Gemma wrapped her arms around Sophie's waist and rested her head against Sophie's side. Tears burned in Awbrey's eyes as she thought about two innocent children being hung. Eddy crouched behind Awbrey and wrapped his arms around her.

"One of the crew went into town when they spotted the smoke yesterday. The man wearing Baron Barnett's owl on his chest had been questioning residents of Ava about anyone using magic," Romke said. He looked around the group, debating on how much to tell. He decided to be blunt. "There was a man who several had long thought could turn into a goat but he was gone. Visiting a relative. So they visited anyone reported to be associated with him. The first children killed were his niece and nephew. Not even of blood. The mother was his deceased wife's sister."

"*The first children*?" Awbrey mouthed.

"A boat," Tucker said.

"A ship," Jaydin said automatically without even looking. The man wiped his eyes.

"Uh, I think it's a boat," Tucker said.

The boy was right. A small boat drifted between them and shore. Two figures were visible sitting in the boat, blankets draped over their shoulders and pulled up over their heads. They drifted at the whim of the river, no oars in sight. One of the crew had also spotted the small vessel. The ship slowed and swung closer to the boat.

"Ahoy, the boat," the captain called down when the boat was aside the ship. "Be ye adrift?

"Are ye friend or foe? If ye be foe I take my chances with the river," the man in the boat asked, raising his head. His face was pale within the shadow created by the blanket. Soot smudges marred his face.

"I be a traveler on the water, friend. Were you in Ava then?" the captain called down.

"Aye," the man said.

"A meal for information then we'll tow you to shore," the

captain said.

"A bargain," the man said in agreement.

Two of the crew immediately lowered a rope ladder, climbed down to the boat and helped the occupants up onto the ship deck. A woman's head appeared at the rail and two crewmen grabbed her arms and lifted her as easily as if she was a feather pillow, gently setting her on her feet. The next face was a young, wide-eyed boy. A crew member appeared at the rail carrying a bundle in the crook of his elbow. The woman reached for the bundle but another burly man was faster, plucking the bundle from his crew mate and handing it to the woman with the greatest care.

The man was the last to reach the rail, a scruffy dog in a bag strapped to his back. The crewmen hoisted him over the rail as smoothly and easily as they had the woman. The second man who had descended into the boat appeared, leaping over the rail with ease. Awbrey watched the crewmen in awe. They moved like everything was a choreographed ballet, with ease and fluid movement.

First a crewman brought a bucket of fresh water with a ladle. This was received gratefully and the man filled the ladle and handed it to the woman. She lowered the ladle over the blanket for a few minutes then put the ladle to the boy's mouth. The woman handed the empty ladle back to the man, who filled it again and passed it back to her. The woman drained the entire ladle then handed it back to the man.

A robust meal was brought up from the galley, enough for the whole group. Another plate of hard biscuits as well as steaming fish and rice seasoned with herbs and fish stock. Even Jaydin refrained from taking from the pot until the refugees had dished up what they wanted, though he licked his lips a few times as he watched them eat.

"We thank you," the man said. "I dropped the oars in the night. I was afraid we would float forever on this river."

Romke nodded at Jaydin and the young man grabbed a plate and filled it with food. The small white dog had crawled onto Sophie's lap. She shared a piece of dried fish left over from their breakfast with the dog. The dog politely took each bite the frail girl offered, patiently waiting until it was his turn to get another piece. Awbrey filled a plate with the warm fish and rice and handed it to Sophie before serving Eddy then herself.

"It was madness," the man said. "The day before yesterday uniformed men rode into town announcing that the king had made a new law, outlawing the use of magic, of being magic."

"We thought it a joke," the woman said, looking up from the bundle in her arms. "Magic? What nonsense!" The bundle cried softly and the woman bounced it up and down gently.

"One of the men wore an owl sigil," the man said. He put another spoonful of rice on the woman's emptied plate and set it beside her. "He was going from house to house warning people that if they knew of anyone magic and did not come forward they would suffer the fate of the magic users."

"That's when the light appeared in the sky. A strange green light pointing right at the center of town," the woman said.

"He was already looking for Jakob by then," the man said to his wife. "Anyway, when the green light appeared the mob took it as a sign. They believed there were magic users amongst us and emotions fired. Since Jakob wasn't within reach they went after anyone connected to Jakob."

Awbrey forced herself not to look at Gemma. She had known that the light display would bring trouble. How far had it been seen? Awbrey could not resist. She stole a quick glance at the girl. Gemma was staring into the pot of fish and rice. The little singer was frozen like a porcelain statue, not even blinking. Jaydin and Sophie were also staring at the girl. Awbrey turned her gaze back to the refugees.

"You are connected to Jakob?" the captain asked.

"He was our neighbor. Our house burnt down when they fired his house. He is a good man, Jakob. It's nonsense that he's a magic user," the man said, shaking his head. "There was no reasoning with the mob though. We escaped before someone remembered that we were friends with our kind neighbor. We already lost everything else, no reason to risk lives."

"Everything was so normal that morning," the woman said softly. "I made oatmeal for breakfast. I put berries and nuts in the oatmeal. Now it's all gone. Just gone. My mother's silver bowl. The cradle my uncle made when Joshin was born. Gone."

Large tears rolled down her cheeks. Her husband wrapped his arms around her and held her tight. The scruffy little dog jumped off Sophie's lap and squirmed between the couple so he could reach the woman's chin with his tongue, somehow managing to be careful not to step on the baby in her arms.

"Where do you go from here?" the captain asked kindly.

"My sister is in Kando," the man said.

"That's only a few hours ahead," the captain said. "We'll drop your boat a few miles out."

"That is kind of you," the man said.

With water and food filling their bellies and the fear of drifting on the river for days in the small boat, the family gradually relaxed. Awbrey had little appetite but eventually managed to eat what was on her plate. Several of the crew collected the dishes and walked away on silent bare feet. Awbrey stared at their feet. It was the first time that she had actually noticed that they wore no shoes.

The boy from the boat and Tucker began to play with a block of wood and a stick. The woman uncovered the baby in order to change his fouled nappy. The woman set the dirty bit of clothe next to her and a crewman immediately snatched it up. He returned in a few minutes and hung the clean but wet diaper on the wire holding the privacy curtain.

"You aren't from Ava," the man said, gaze on Jaydin.

"We were passing Ava and saw the fires," the captain said.

The man nodded, finding his fellow travelers interesting now that he was feeling safer. His gaze lingered on Sophie. His wife was also staring at Sophie. The two exchanged glances. The woman nodded at the man.

"Since you have helped us I will warn you," the man said. "The man with the owl sigil was asking about a slender blonde girl. A lot like you. A Garlan he said. You look like a Garlan."

"How strange," Sophie said in a cold voice. "Do you get a lot of visitors from Garlan in Ava?"

"No, not so much. But I've been to Garlan," the man said.

"Did you bring anyone from Garlan back with you?" Sophie asked. The man shook his head, looking uncomfortable. "Well that's odd then, isn't it? That this man would be looking for someone from Garlan in Ava."

"He's trying to help," Jaydin said to Sophie.

She bent her head for a moment then looked up at the man. "I apologize. I did not mean to be disrespectful. Thank you for warning us that the man leading the mob is looking for someone who matches my description." She was sincere.

"And a girl with dark hair," the woman said, looking directly at Awbrey.

"Me?" Awbrey asked in surprise.

"Lots of girls have dark hair," Eddy said lightly to Awbrey. "A girl with dark hair is as generic a description as you can get."

Awbrey laughed. "Of course. It was just that, well, never mind. I know he couldn't mean me because I have never met or even seen any baron. Er, or anyone from the baron who would be looking for me. Or, I mean, why would he be looking for me?"

"He wouldn't be," Eddy said. "Here, eat a biscuit."

Awbrey took the biscuit from Eddy but did not eat it. She knew that she was rambling but when that woman had said that he was looking for a dark haired girl and stared directly at her, it had made her feel that the woman knew that he had reason to be hunting for her.

"Did he say why he was looking for these girls?" Romke asked.

The couple shook their heads. "It was at the docks. When things had run their course. Men in uniform were at the docks looking for the Garlan girl," the man said.

"It was when the mob started out, every dark haired girl he saw he would look at and shake his head and say not her," the woman said.

"Oh, I am not from Ava," Awbrey said, visibly relieved. "It wasn't me he was looking for after all." She glanced up at Eddy, who frowned at her. "Not that I thought it was me. It's just, well, never mind."

"Well, I hope he does not find the girls he is looking for. I fear he does not have good intentions towards them," Romke said. A breeze blew over the ship's deck and Awbrey shivered.

Eventually the captain returned. "We're nearing Kando," he said.

The crewmen assisted the family down into their small boat and handed down two wood staves from a barrel to use as oars to get them to shore. Rope had been securely wrapped around one end of each makeshift oar to provide firm grip. The man and woman each took a makeshift oar and rowed away from the ship toward shore. The crew watched the boat until it touched shore. The man climbed out and pulled the boat out of the water then waved at the ship. The crew waved back and then went back to their tasks.

The small town of Kando was visible around the next bend in the river. There were a lot of bends in the river, as with most rivers. There was no sign of destruction in this town. Brightly painted houses lined a hill above the river, far enough back to stay out of reach of a rising spring river. Awbrey had not realized she had been holding her breath until she let it out when she saw that the town looked intact.

"Look," Awbrey said, pointing. A group of uniformed men sat on horseback on a rise, watching the river. It was not really a hill but was the highest point outside of the town.

"No pointing," Romke said. "Stay below the rail."

Chapter Nine

The ship sailed past Kando in a matter of minutes. It was not a large town. The uniformed watchers did not find the ship interesting. The men sat on their horses, glancing at the ship but it did not hold their gaze. Their focus was on the river but they apparently watched for more interesting game to come.

Awbrey took a deep breath in relief, though she was not sure what the men could have done to stop the ship from flowing past while they sat on their horses on the bank above. The captain was smart to have put the refugees ashore before reaching Kando. If the ship had been closer to shore the uniformed riders might have been more interested and interfered with their passing.

"Two more days to Green Falls," Romke muttered, watching the mounted party of uniformed men slide further into the distance.

"Then what?" Eddy asked.

"We take the Old Road east," Romke said.

"East? To Summit? Why not stay on the river into Iberland. It is a shorter course to leave the country," Eddy said.

"Baron Barnett will expect that. I am sure he will have soldiers posted there and at Delta," Romke said. "He will have a watchful eye set at such key locations. He won't suspect Summit."

"Why would he?" Eddy asked. "It's a horrible route."

"River's too high for this ship," the captain said. "It's called Green Falls for a reason."

"I thought a ship could sail north to Iberland," Eddy said.

"Aye. But not this flat-bottomed beast," the captain said.

"Then why use this flat-bottomed beast in the first place?" Eddy asked in frustration.

"Had to carry a monster of a wagon and four horses," the captain said.

"But why--" Eddy began to say.

"The plan was to leave the river at Green Falls," Romke interrupted. "That's that."

Eddy grunted in frustration but did not pursue the topic. He stared out across the river for a very long time, deep in thought. The captain went back to his tasks and Romke stiffly walked away as well. Awbrey watched Eddy. It was as if he was trying to see what lay ahead by sheer force of will. Or a lot of patience.

Something felt familiar about Eddy and fast moving whitewater but she could not place the memory. It was like she had already lived the moment but she knew that she had not. A shiver ran down Awbrey's spine and she gave a little shake. Though her father had talked often of Green River she had never been there.

"What do you see, Eddy?" Awbrey asked, slipping her arm into the crook of his elbow and leaning her cheek against his arm.

Eddy looked down at her. He blinked. "See? Nothing actually. I'm thinking."

"What are you thinking then?" Awbrey asked.

"If it's possible to get this ship through the falls," Eddy said.

"They portage some ships in early summer," Awbrey said. "It's funny because you would think that the river running high would make it easier but it's the opposite."

"I don't understand," Eddy said.

"I don't either. I remember my father talking about it with one of his customers years ago. I think he was trying to explain the higher cost. I guess I remember because it didn't make sense," Awbrey said.

"Maybe because the water runs faster when it's higher," Eddy said thoughtfully.

"Perhaps," Awbrey said in agreement. Awbrey glanced around them. They had as much privacy as was possible on a ship. No one was within hearing range. "What's it like to be magic, Eddy? And why did you never tell me?"

"I would have told you eventually. I tried a few times. Sometimes I would forget that you didn't know. I'm so used to telling you everything that sometimes you are just part of me," Eddy said.

"But what does it feel like? How did you know that you are magic?" Awbrey asked looking up at him.

Eddy shrugged. "I can't explain it. Besides, you should know what it is to be magic."

"I don't do anything that is magic," Awbrey said in frustration. She slipped her arm out of Eddy's arm and leaned over the guard rail. "You wave your hand and unbelievable things happen. That's magic. Jaydin can turn into animals. That's magic. Gemma sings and things happen. That's magic. Sophie can talk to animals. I don't do anything."

"You must. Or you wouldn't be here," Eddy said.

"I think it's a mistake."

"We have had this conversation already, Awbrey," Eddy said. "Your reading dreams. That's a talent. I know. I know," Eddy said before she could protest. "It's just symbols. But you *know* when you hear a dream. You know. Did you practice with the others as we discussed?"

"It doesn't do any good. I tried to look into what more I could do by reading everyone's dreams yesterday morning and all I did was make everyone angry with me," Awbrey said.

Eddy leaned his back against the rail next to her and crossed his legs. "I'm sure they aren't angry. Maybe you surprised them with what you saw. It's easy to mistake surprise and anger."

"I miss my home. I miss my parents," Awbrey said, staring out at the trees as they slid away in the opposite direction. "Will life ever go back to normal? When we get to where we're going?"

"It will be our new normal," Eddy said. He nodded his head when Sophie approached them. Awbrey looked over her shoulder and watched Sophie walking toward them.

"You two, always snuggling up together away from everyone else," Sophie said in greeting. She smiled up at Eddy. "Is she whining about not being magic and just wanting to go home again?"

Awbrey frowned. First, they barely managed to get any time alone and alone was not even really alone when there was someone always within sight. As far as whining, she was not whining. Awbrey wondered if Sophie had heard them talking to know the topic. Sophie must have been eavesdropping because she could not have wildly guessed the exact discussion they had been having.

"We were just discussing our life ahead," Eddy said with a smile. Sophie frowned and glanced at Awbrey. Awbrey gave Sophie her biggest smile, fake though it was.

"Ah, yes. Life ahead. Hopefully we get to Garlan intact," Sophie said with a sweet, demure smile. "When we get to Garlan we will have to convince the king to allow us to stay."

"Oh, I am sure that if we can't stay in Garlan we can move on to someplace else," Eddy said. "I think the goal is just to get out of Kiel now."

"Did you want something, Sophie?" Awbrey asked.

"Just to join the discussion," Sophie said. She leaned against the rail on the other side of Eddy. "I am bored."

"Enjoy the boredom while it lasts," Eddy said.

Sophie grew somber immediately. "I can't stop thinking about Ava. Imagine all the people of a town turning on each other. What drives people to do that?" Sophie sidled right up next to Eddy and looked up at him with a long face. "It grieves me so."

Awbrey turned her head and stared back out over the river. She leaned forward with her forearms resting on the rail. Awbrey wanted to forget about Ava and all those burnt houses. The smell still stuck in her nose. Awbrey thought about the mob of people hanging innocent children. It was too horrible to think about.

Nothing could quite dispel the image of the carnage that swept through Ava. The burnt buildings and smoking rubble represented how a few moments could change people's lives forever. Those were people's homes and livelihoods gone in one chaotic night. Awbrey skirted away from the thought of people losing their lives as well.

Children killed because their uncle was rumored to possibly be magic was difficult for Awbrey to comprehend. It was wrong. It was so horribly wrong. Thinking about it twisted her stomach into knot, so she avoided thinking about it at all.

Awbrey looked up at Eddy. He looked uncomfortable with Sophie pressing herself up against him. Awbrey almost smiled. Eddy looked at Awbrey, rolling his eyes back towards Sophie, who was clutching his arm now. Awbrey nodded and jerked her head at Sophie. Eddy sighed and put his arm around the frail, blonde girl and patted her shoulder.

Sophie took a deep breath and started crying. Eddy's eyes widened and he looked ready to bolt but he stayed where he was. Awbrey smiled warmly at her Eddy. She knew that Sophie just needed a hug. The frail, blonde girl tried to put on a hard front but she was scared. They were all scared.

Eventually Sophie straightened and wiped her eyes. "Thank you, Eddy. It's just when I think of those poor children. Oh, those poor children. If we had been in Ava it would be us hanging on the dock."

Eddy looked uncomfortable. He removed his arm from Sophie's shoulders. "Romke will get us to safety. I will do my best to protect everyone as well."

"That girl will do whatever it takes to survive this," Eddy said, frowning as he watched Sophie wander away.

"I think it was nice of you to comfort her," Awbrey said.

Eddy looked down at Awbrey thoughtfully. He pulled her closer to him and rested his chin on her head. "I love you, Awbrey. I think it was nice of you to think she was looking for comfort."

"What do you mean? Of course she was just looking for a hug. What else?" Awbrey said.

"She was flexing her muscles," Eddy said.

Awbrey thought about that. She looked up at Eddy in surprise. "You think she wants to steal you away from me?"

Eddy shook his head. "No. Just see how far she can push. She is already jealous of you and I am a toy she wants just because I belong to you. No other reason."

"Pff. What nonsense. Jealous of me? She's really a princess, you know. I can believe that she would fall for your charm and great looks but it's you I trust. So don't go breaking her heart. But there's nothing wrong with giving her a shoulder. Ava still haunts my thoughts, even this minute. It was hard on her as well," Awbrey said.

"Not in the same way as it's hard on you," Eddy said. "You care about those people. She cares about the impact on her. That's different."

"Don't you like Sophie?" Awbrey asked in surprise.

"It's not a matter of liking. I just like to see things as they are," Eddy said.

The ship sailed on north. That night the captain pulled in closer to shore and dropped anchor. Clouds obscured the moonlight and he did not want to risk running into something in the dark. Several crew members rowed to shore in a small boat that had been attached to the side of the ship.

The travelers hauled up buckets of water and bathed the best they could behind their curtained areas. Awbrey cringed at the coldness of the water but it was too dangerous for Gemma to perform her little warm waterfall song again. The last thing they needed was for someone to see water magically flowing up to the boat and back down again. The effort had also worn Gemma out. The girl had slept most of the afternoon. So everyone cleaned critical areas and suffered the cold. After they spot cleaned themselves they washed their dirty underclothes and hung them to dry.

Dawn brought a pink horizon and the ship moving along the center of the river again. The sound of the ship creaking as it moved through the water and the river lapping against the ship's sides was almost relaxing. Awbrey preferred riding on the river over sitting cooped up inside the swaying, rumbling wagon.

"Do you want to hear our dreams this morning?" Sophie asked Awbrey while they ate breakfast. It was only the four of them again. Eddy was visiting with the captain and Tucker was shadowing Romke as usual. The boy had decided at some point to never be more than a few feet from the older man.

"Only if you want to," Awbrey said warily. The first try had not gone over very well.

"Me first. Me first," Gemma said.

"Go ahead," Awbrey said.

"I had a dream that a man came out of the river and warned us that the river ahead was going to take life. But when he spoke it was all squeals and strange sounds. No one could understand him but you," Gemma said. "I tried to sing his words into sense but when I started to sing he jumped back into the river. The river had turned all white and moved angrily."

Awbrey stared at the girl. It took a few minutes for Awbrey to find her voice. "Can you swim, Gemma?"

Gemma shook her head. "No. At least I don't know because I've never tried."

"Jaydin, can you swim?" Awbrey asked. Jaydin nodded. "Stay near Gemma."

"You think it's me? You think I'll drown?" Gemma asked.

Excitement warred with fear on her face.

"I think that it's good that you brought it to attention that you can't swim. Few dreams predict the future but often they warn the dreamer of details the dreamer has missed while awake," Awbrey said.

The first thought Awbrey had upon hearing Gemma's dream was that instead of being a dream it was something that had actually happened and woken Gemma in the night but the girl remembered the incident as a dream. If a creature of the river was trying to warn of danger ahead, it puzzled Awbrey that it chose Gemma as the messenger. Awbrey had never heard of people living in rivers yet it did not feel like a dream.

Gemma stared out at the wide expanse of water surrounding them, deeply considering Awbrey's words. She frowned as she pondered the dream. "Maybe he would have said more if I had not tried to sing at him," the girl said thoughtfully.

"I dreamt that I was in a house, a palace really. There was a door in the bedroom that I had never noticed before. When I opened the door there were more rooms, mostly dirty and dusty from disuse. Big rooms, little rooms, all these rooms that somehow appeared where they couldn't be," Sophie said.

"How did you feel?" Awbrey asked.

"Feel?"

"About finding the rooms," Awbrey said,

"Excited," Sophie said after reflection. "It was so exciting to have so many extra rooms."

"You have talents you have not used fully," Awbrey said. "Those rooms represent areas of your mind."

"You mean like talking to inanimate objects as well?" Sophie asked.

"I think more like sewing or drawing," Awbrey said.

Sophie stared at Awbrey then laughed. "One of the rooms had an easel and canvas. I remember now thinking in the dream that the lighting was perfect for painting."

Eddy approached them. He crouched next to Awbrey. "There's something ahead. A raft or debris from Ava most likely." He looked at each of them. "Try to stay below the guard rail."

"Did you see people?" Sophie asked even as Gemma jumped to her feet and leaned over the guard rail in an attempt to see what was ahead on the river.

Eddy nodded. "Figures. No movement."

The crew scurried about, pulling ropes, pushing beams, and climbing. The sails dropped, flapping in the wind until they were secured. The ship slowed. A burly man dropped the anchor. The ship vibrated and rattled for a moment as the heavy piece of stone dragged the chain it was attached to out of a box bolted on the rear deck. The ship slowed even more quickly. If Awbrey had not been sitting down she would have fallen.

Awbrey peered over the guard rail nearest them. There was no sign of a raft but charred wood and some other debris floated in the water. One of the crew dropped a ladder on the other side of the ship and gracefully vaulted over the guard rail. Awbrey cringed. Though watching them move about the ship at their tasks was like watching a dance, there were times like this, vaulting blindly over the side of the ship that Awbrey thought that maybe they might be a little too confident in their physical abilities.

The urge to see was strong. Awbrey moved to get to her feet, unable to resist curiosity. Eddy put his hand on her arm and shook his head.

"You don't want to see this, Awbrey," he said in a low voice.

"Maybe I need to see, Eddy," she replied.

Sophie and Jaydin had also scrambled to their feet and were walking to the other side of the ship with bent backs in an attempt to stay low. Eddy shook his head. Awbrey hesitated then got to her feet. She looked around the ship. Nothing human or even human made was in sight along the shore. Awbrey walked with a straight back to where the others gathered by the guard rail. The wind carried the scent of the horse pen to that side of the ship.

Below them was a piece of charred fencing lashed to two barrels. One of the crewmen was carefully making his way between the bundles of clothes lying on the makeshift raft. He placed his bare foot down, gave a little twist on the ball of his foot then put his weight on that foot. He stretched his leg out, placed his bare foot on an open piece of wood, gave his foot a twist and stepped over. The makeshift raft bobbed up and down with each step he took.

Two small bundles and an adult human sized bundle lay on the raft. The raft rose and sank as the man leaned down and checked the first bundle but he remained standing, his legs matching the rocking motion of the raft. He moved aside some of the cloth and placed his hand inside. He held that position for several minutes then pulled his hand back. He looked up at the captain and shook his head.

"Damn," the captain muttered.

Everyone watched silently as the burly man gingerly stepped around on the precarious raft to reach each of the other two bundles and check for signs of life. After checking each one he looked up and shook his head. Awbrey held her breath as she watched the brave sailor. After finding no sign of life in the third bundle he straightened and waited for the captain's order, legs subtly shifting up and down with the rocking of the piece of fencing.

"We have to leave them," Romke said.

"We canna just leave them," the captain said, appalled.

"We don't have time to go to shore and bury them and a pyre will just draw attention," Romke said.

Romke looked at Eddy, who had followed Awbrey and stood at her shoulder. The look was questioning. Eddy nodded once, the barest jerk of his chin. Awbrey's chin quivered as she realized that all three people on the raft were dead.

There was shouting below. The crewman on the raft tried to hold his balance as the makeshift raft rocked back and forth. Several small eddies were visible in the water ahead of the raft, swirling circles of water barely two feet in diameter. The rope attaching the two barrels to the ends of the fencing had given way. The barrels floated free, spinning as they hit the swirling water then popping free only to be caught briefly in the next eddy.

The fence wobbled even more drastically on the river. The crewman on the raft leaped for the rope ladder just in time as the fence fell apart and the figures slid into the river and out of sight. The burly man hung from the rope ladder and looked over his shoulder at the sinking raft with its mysterious load of three. He shook his head and clambered up the rope ladder.

"Looks like chance stepped in," the captain muttered. "Raise those sails! We have a deadline."

Awbrey buried her face against Eddy's shoulder. Her knees felt weak. Those small bundles were children. Innocent children. Dead for no reason. Awbrey felt sorrow for the adult as well, not knowing if it was a mother or a father trying to save their children. It was just that the loss of the children hit her so much harder.

Eddy put his arms around her, comforting her as she cried for the loss of the children and their parent. He stroked her hair as she cried. "It isn't right," she whispered.

"Truly, it is sad," Eddy agreed.

"Those poor souls are lost, lost in the depths of the river. Vanished without even knowing who they were," Awbrey said, taking a deep breath. "Their family will never know what has become of them."

Gemma continued to stare down at the water where the raft had sank, head turning to keep the spot in sight as the ship began to move again. The girl did not cry but she was clearly impacted by the incident. As the ship moved farther downstream the girl walked along the ship's side, trying to hold the spot with her gaze. She stared back at the river long past when the spot was visible any longer, deep in her thoughts.

Eventually Sophie wiped her eyes and walked over to Gemma. The frail, blonde girl put her arm around Gemma's shoulders and gave her a hug. Sophie bent her head and talked to Gemma for several minutes. Gemma shook her head from shoulder to shoulder. Sophie continued to talk but Awbrey could not hear what was said. After several minutes listening to Sophie, Gemma finally nodded and turned, walking back to the center of the deck.

"Strange coincidence," Jaydin said, coming up next to Awbrey and Eddy but looking at Sophie and Gemma.

"What is?" Awbrey asked.

"That Romke did not want to stop to deal with the bodies and the raft conveniently fell apart a few minutes later, removing the problem," Jaydin said, looking at Eddy now.

"Why strange? It was a precarious raft," Eddy said. "It's fortunate that the crewman did not take a dunking. Fascinating balance these men have. I wouldn't be surprised if they could run over water as well."

"I still think it's an odd coincidence," Jaydin said. "Those people were denied a proper burial. It isn't right."

"You saw that raft, Jaydin," Eddy said. "Would you have stepped down onto it?"

Jaydin considered. After thinking it over he shook his head no. "It was very daring and brave for that crewman to walk on it. Every minute he was standing there my heart was in my throat expecting him to plunge into the river. I just thought, well, Romke really wanted to avoid dealing with it and then the problem was gone."

"Perhaps we could say a few words, in memorial," Eddy suggested.

The small group of travelers gathered at the guard rail where the rope ladder had been dropped over the side to investigate the raft. Though they had left behind the actual burial location in the river, the spot at the guard rail felt appropriate. The smell of horse dung was stronger now and a few flies flew around their heads. The captain and several of the burly crew joined the group when they realized what they were doing. Everyone stood facing the river.

"We don't know who you were, only suspecting you lost your way while escaping the horror that took Ava in its grip a few nights back," Romke said, head bowed low. "Be ye at peace now. Know that the pain is over, the fear is at rest, and the spirit is free to soar. Be ye at peace."

One of the crewmen began to sing. Awbrey jumped in surprise. It was a sad lament. It did not take long for the rest of the crew to join in the song. The voices were deep and filled with sadness as the men sang of a frozen land where all must visit whether they were ready or not. The song sent shivers down Awbrey's spine. The song was not long and ended with the solo voice of the same man who had started the song, singing one last verse. The burly crew stood with their heads down for a full minute then dispersed.

"I thought they were mutes," Sophie said in a low voice to Eddy and Awbrey. Maybe she just said it to Eddy but Awbrey was standing right there as well,

"It is the first time I heard any of them utter a word," Awbrey said in agreement.

Sophie glanced at Awbrey as if not realizing that she was there until she spoke then walked away. For some reason Awbrey had the urge to stick her tongue out at the frail, blonde girl as she walked to stand beside Romke but she resisted. It would not be appropriate behavior at a memorial service.

As they neared Green Falls the river narrowed and deepened. The soft banks changed to hard rock worn smooth by countless years of rushing water flowing over it. The first signs of the town could be seen in the distance along the eastern bank. A spire rose, a silhouette against a blue sky.

Small farms were now visible, scattered near and far. They became more closely clustered the closer they came to Green Falls. Rope or wood ladders hung on both sides of the rock shores, providing access to small docks that either floated tethered to the rock or were more firmly secured to the rock face with great metal bolts. Houses were visible on both sides of the river near the docks.

More debris floated in the river, mostly charred wood, whether it be timbers or large sections of fencing or walls. A few people were visible going about their business, feeding chickens, gathering rocks in a small field, or hanging wash on a line. A few waved at the ship but most did not even notice it passing.

"We will pull up to the south dock," the captain said to Romke, pointing to a vague location ahead of them on the river.

They rounded another bend in the river and the captain brought out a spy glass to study the shore ahead. A small dock wobbled and bobbed on the river, one end tethered to the rock with ropes as thick as a crewman's arm. The captain edged the ship up to the dock and the sails were dropped. Two crewmen adroitly dropped onto the dock from the ship's side.

"You really don't expect even your men to unload the wagon here," Romke said in surprise, staring at the dock.

"Ach," the captain said, shaking his head and laughing.

The two men trotted across the dock and clambered up the wood ladder bolted on the bank's side. They vanished from sight quickly. Once they were gone the captain dropped anchor. The dock would not be capable of supporting the ship if they had tied up to it. They waited.

"How will we get the wagon up these banks?" Sophie asked, studying the area.

"They are not this high further north. The town's dock," the captain said. "But even so we'll still need the crane."

"A crane?" Sophie asked.

"A winch on tracks. They'll raise the wagon then swing it over," the captain said, moving his hands to show things raising and sliding sideways.

"I could do that," Gemma said eagerly.

"No!" Romke and the captain said in unison.

"Someone would see," Romke added before Gemma could protest. "So far no one knows we are anything but simple travelers."

"Except the angry man with the club," Gemma pointed out.

"We could make our own crane so it looks like we are just using a crane," Jaydin said.

"Then anyone seeing us would wonder why we are avoiding the city's dock," the captain said.

"Then why are we just sitting here?" Sophie asked.

"To make sure we don't have reason to avoid the city dock," the captain said.

"Patience, children," Romke said.

They waited for several hours before the two burly men returned to the ship. The two men had a brief discussion aside with the captain. The sun was on a downward slide to the horizon now. The captain frowned as he listened to his men then nodded. The anchor was raised and the ship moved out into the river's current once again. The sails were raised and the ship raced toward Green Falls.

The next bend in the river showed more of the town but it was still quite a distance away. Awbrey realized the two crewmen must have run all the way into town and back again. A steady roar was discernible in the distance. Awbrey made her way to the front of the ship and stared ahead.

The roar was coming from the river. Rainbows and sparkles danced across the river beyond the town. Boulders peeked up from the water. Where the river poured over the boulders the water was churned into white froth. The spray created from all the churning and motion caught the low sun's light, causing the sparkle and dancing colors.

The sight of the white water in the distance held her attention. Awbrey had never visited Green Falls yet something about the river here felt familiar, as well as scary. It felt like she had already lived this moment though she knew that she had not. Something tickled the back of her brain, some elusive memory. Awbrey looked back over her shoulder. Romke stood nearby, talking to Eddy. Eddy leaned down to hear the older man over the river's roar.

Awbrey shivered. There was something she should remember about Romke and Eddy on white water. There was danger for Eddy on white water. The town's south dock was visible ahead and to the right side. The crane stood tall on shore. The white water churning and roaring ahead was well beyond the dock but Awbrey felt a keen sense of danger.

Chapter Ten

The captain guided the ship up to the city dock and the burly crew rushed about to secure the ship. A ramp was dropped over the side where a section of the guard rail swung aside on hinges. Seagulls flew overhead, their annoying loud cries filling the air around the dock. Two birds landed on the guard rail, watching the work being done. The crew led the horses down the ramp even as Romke gestured for everyone in their group to disembark as well.

"It will take time to unload the wagon and I need to oversee that. Go to the Flagon Inn. It's nearby," Romke said. He handed Eddy a small stack of coins. "Get two rooms and reserve the bath house. If I haven't joined you by then order dinner served in a private room."

The small group clustered together at the end of the dock, looking around them. Though it was evening it was still light out and the area bustled with people going about their business. Ships did not always arrive on a set schedule so dock workers and city officials were often at the dock at odd hours.

Seagulls were everywhere, screeching as they flew overhead. A man cleaning fish tossed the refuse aside and the gulls swarmed the ground where the innards landed, when a lucky gull did not manage to snatch the guts in the air. A few flew out of the cluster carrying bits of fish guts in their bills. More flew after the winners, trying to steal the bite of food. Awbrey watched the man working at his slatted table, amazed that the seagulls did not try to steal the fish from his table right out of his hands.

Jaydin started walking from the dock into town. The rest of the group automatically followed him. The Flagon Inn was easy to find. The sign was visible within a few feet beyond the dock, a large ceramic carafe painted on a white washed board hanging on the corner of the second floor. The small group of youngsters barely earned a second look from pedestrians around the dock as they made their way toward the inn.

They must have looked quite the sight, walking with their heads bobbing and turning, eyes wide as they tried to absorb everything they saw. Jaydin and Eddy were not as overwhelmed as the girls but even Jaydin stopped in his tracks when he saw a trio of scantily clad women lounging in front of a building with a sign proclaiming that they were passing the Traveling Man's Refuge.

One of the women noticed Jaydin and stepped away from the building. She twirled slowly with her arms above her head, turning her head to watch Jaydin over her shoulder as she twirled. The woman smiled seductively. The dress she wore was transparent and her red under garments were clearly visible through the gossamer fabric. Jaydin turned red and hurried ahead.

Awbrey looked up at Eddy, who walked at her side, intending to ask him what it meant. Eddy was staring at the women with wide eyes. "Eddy," she hissed.

"What? Uh, keep walking," Eddy muttered.

"Do you think they are beautiful?" Awbrey asked.

"Well they are sure dressed to attract attention," Eddy said quickly.

The crewmen leading the horses were ahead of them and had headed directly to the stable on the side of the Flagon Inn. Eddy paused to look at the men with his horse but everything looked to be in control so Eddy kept going to the inn door.

There was a man behind a desk to greet anyone entering the inn. Eddy strode purposely up to the desk and politely but firmly requested two rooms, the bath house, and meals for seven served in a private dining room in an hour. The man looked at the group thoughtfully then nodded.

"Roast pork and rice tonight," the clerk said as he pulled two keys from a board behind the desk. "For an added mark there's fowl available as well."

"We'll take the fowl also," Jaydin said, stepping up to the desk.

The clerk nodded as he handed the two room keys to Eddy. He pulled another key from a drawer in the desk and handed that to Eddy as well. "Bath house. Girls to the right. Boys to the left. When you are done dinner will be waiting for you in the red room."

"Red room?" Eddy asked.

"Door's red. Right there," the clerk said, pointing. To their right was a large common area filled with tables and people. An oak bar ran the length of one wall and two men in white stood behind the bar to serve refreshments to guests and townspeople looking for a meal or beer. There were three doors between the clerk's desk and the common room, a red door, green door, and brown door. "Bath house is in back. Through that door." The clerk pointed in the other direction, down a hall with numbered doors.

Eddy paid the man when he named a fair price. Everyone else headed for the bath house while Eddy was counting out coins from the coin purse Romke had given him. They walked down the hallway and had to wait for Eddy so he could unlock the door.

Heat and steam assaulted them as soon as Eddy opened the door. The room was large but had a low ceiling. Little cubbies with curtains lined the back wall. An attendant waited with robes at a desk similar to the front clerk's desk. He handed each of them a robe so he could take their clothes.

This concept of stripping off their clothes to give to him created some small confusion but the attendant quickly explained that they could remove their clothes in the curtained closets behind him, put on the robe, and give him their clothes when they came out. The clothes would be cleaned and waiting when they came out of the bath house.

"Not takin' my clothes," Tucker muttered, hugging his arms around his waist to prevent anyone from removing his clothes.

"They need cleaning," Eddy said, pushing Tucker into the curtained closet. "Strip and hand them over."

"No," Tucker yelled from inside the changing closet.

"If you don't hand out those clothes I will drag you out here and strip you down in front of everyone," Eddy warned. Within minutes a small hand appeared holding out a shirt. "All of it, Tucker. Put on the robe after you've taken it all off and come out with your clothes." He looked over at Awbrey. "You don't have to wait for us. Go head to the girls' room."

Being clean and wearing clean clothes put everyone in a good mood. Tucker was convinced that they had used magic to return clean, dry clothes in the time it took them to bathe despite Sophie explaining that they used heated metal plates to dry the clothes. Awbrey was impressed that all the clothes were properly returned, nothing mixed up.

Romke arrived with the food. Three waiters entered the red room with trays of covered bowls shortly after they entered the room and Romke followed on the heels of the waiters. The waiters set the bowls in a line in the center of the table. When the waiters removed the lids, steam rose up from the bowls, filling the room with smells that made the stomach rumble in hunger.

The waiters left the room but one returned almost immediately with a tray of fowls. Two ducks and a goose roosted to perfection were revealed when he lifted the lid and set the tray on the table. For a moment everyone stared in awe at the bountiful feast. After a few days of eating hard biscuits and dried or fresh fish, the food on the table looked fit to feed a king.

In unison everyone grabbed a flat bowl and spooned roast pork, gravy, red cabbage, marinated asparagus, cooked beets, and rice cooked in broth with carrots, onions, and seasoning. No one talked for several minutes except to request a specific dish passed down.

"I have never tasted anything so good," Jaydin said, closing his eyes as he bit into another piece of roast pork.

"Rooms aren't the best but the food here makes up for it," Romke said. "Should have warned you to pass on the fowl. Let me guess, Jaydin chimed in? You can eat them for breakfast."

"I didn't know there would be so much food," Jaydin admitted.

Only Jaydin was still eating, trying his best to clean a duck carcass, when two waiters entered the room again. They carried covered trays, which they set on the sideboard. They removed any empty dish, one waiter stacking the dishes in the arms of the other waiter. The waiter carrying the empty dishes left the room and the remaining waiter moved the two new trays onto the center of the table. He pulled small plates out of the sideboard and set the stack of plates on the table then uncovered the trays and left the room.

There was stunned silence as the youngsters stared in awe at the selection of desserts sitting on the trays. There was cake decorated with almonds. There were cookies crusted with sugar. There were lemon bars, date bars, and custard tarts. Jaydin groaned.

Clean and with full bellies, they retired to their rooms. The rooms were not side by side but were across the hall from each other. The two rooms were almost identical, small, with two beds jammed into the cramped space. One of the rooms had two full-sized beds and one room had a full-sized bed and a smaller bed. The girls went into the room with one and a half beds and the men into the other room.

One of the beds was full sized but the second bed was little more than a cot. Awbrey and Sophie played evens-odds to see who got to share the bigger bed with Gemma. Sophie won the bigger bed shared with Gemma. Awbrey sat on the small bed against the wall, bouncing a little to judge its comfort. She heard a pop under the mattress and stopped bouncing.

"What will we do when we reach Garlan?" Awbrey asked, plumping the pillow by beating it.

"Sleep for a week on a real bed," Sophie said, stripping down to her under things. The chemise she wore had pink ribbons on it. She slid under the covers next to Gemma. "I think you got the better bed."

Awbrey removed her nicely cleaned dress and hung it on a hook above the bed. Awbrey laid down on the small bed, her feet dangling over the edge. "I doubt it. I think it only has high expectations of becoming a bed one day. For now I shall call it a cot."

Sophie giggled. "At least we aren't on something that's moving. I swear I still feel like everything is moving around me."

"It is worth it to not have to sleep in my clothes," Awbrey said, sighing. The mattress was lumpy but the sheets were crisp and clean.

"I will sleep on a bed the size of this room and sleep in satin pajamas," Sophie said wistfully. "I miss my bed. Isn't it funny how much you take things for granted? A bed. I never realized how great it was to have a real bed."

"Won't Baron Barnett hunt us in Garlan as well?" Awbrey asked. She sat up and pounded her fist into the pillow again.

"He can't," Sophie said. "My, uh, the king won't allow him in the country."

"Well, if he's hunting us because he thinks its evil to be magic, wouldn't he try? What good to just chase magic users out of Kiel?" Awbrey asked, lying down again.

"You ask complicated questions, Awbrey. It's enough to try to reach Garlan in one piece. We aren't there yet," Sophie said. "Gemma fell asleep before her head hit the bed. We should do the same. Romke does like to hit the road before the sun."

"Sophie?"

"Yes?"

"I know you are the Garlan princess. Why try to hide it?" Awbrey asked.

Sophie sighed. "Yes. I just wanted to forget for a while. I just wanted to be normal for a change. You are so lucky."

"Me? Lucky?" Awbrey asked in surprise.

"You grew up in a loving home. Your parents care about you. To my father I am just an asset. You are so beautiful. Men are nice to you and they smile when they look at you. Men just want to use me. You have Eddy. I have never seen two people so in love. Real love," Sophie said, a hint of anger creeping into her voice. "I just wish for that."

The room was too dark to see more than the general shape of the bed with two lumps on top of it. Awbrey was so amazed that she was speechless. Sophie was jealous of her? It was impossible. Eddy had guessed it though. Awbrey wondered how Eddy had known.

Sophie was a beautiful young woman, so frail with such striking blonde hair. Sophie was a princess, which meant that she was pampered and must have tons of servants to see to her every whim, not just sweet, old Jane. Sophie would marry a prince one day and have little princes and princesses and live in a castle. How could she ever be jealous of Awbrey?"

"Baron Barnett is determined to catch me because I refused him. Do you know what that means, Awbrey?" Sophie laughed. "Actually, never mind. You probably don't know what that means. You are so protected and naïve. I was visiting Lethbridge because there were negotiations going on about my possibly being wed to Eldrid. I won't have a choice in who I wed. I will never have the love you and Eddy have." Sophie grew quiet for several minutes before continuing. "Baron Barnett spoiled the negotiations because he wanted me for himself."

"What will he do if he catches you?" Awbrey asked, sitting up. "Will he try to marry you?"

Sophie laughed. "I am amazed at you. He wasn't trying to marry me, Awbrey. He hates magic users but he still lusted after me."

"But, but you're a princess," Awbrey said, shocked into losing her words.

"I am the daughter of a king he has no respect for. If he thought to gain something by marrying me he would rid himself of his wife to do so. But he would gain nothing. I am fourth in line, you see. My eldest brother recently wed and before long I will move farther and farther down the line."

"I don't understand at all," Awbrey said. "How can he think, well, you are a princess."

"He is a man who thinks he can do anything he wants," Sophie said. "I am but a girl with a title. Have you really never encountered anyone such as him? You are a pretty girl. Surely some man has thought to take advantage of you."

"No. Never," Awbrey said, shaking her head.

"I find that hard to believe," Sophie said, a hard edge to her voice again. "There are always men trying to get their hands on pretty, young girls such as you."

"You say I am naïve but to me you sound quite bitter. I think men like Baron Barnett are rare, not common," Awbrey said. Awbrey had never encountered anyone who wanted to take advantage of her. She wondered if it was something maybe Sophie did?

"He is not the only one. He is just one who has the power to destroy kingdoms to get what he wants," Sophie said.

"Did you maybe do something that made him think you shared his regard?" Awbrey asked.

Sophie hissed, a sharp intake of breath. "Again, I will allow that you are naïve. No! I did not share his, what did you call it, regard?"

Awbrey considered Sophie's words. "You think he has done this just to get you, get you lustfully?" she asked in amazement. "People have had their lives destroyed. People have died. Children have died."

"That's not my fault," Sophie said, voice catching. "It's not my fault."

Awbrey slipped out from under the covers and went to the bed Sophie shared with Gemma. Using her hands she found the edge of the bed and sat down next to Sophie. She hugged the frail, blonde girl. "Of course it's not your fault. How can you even think so? It is Baron Barnett's fault for making such a law. It is the fault of those who are so quick to turn their backs on their friends and neighbors. Baron didn't do this because of you. He did this because of him."

"I tell myself that," Sophie said, sobbing. "But I feel like it's all my fault. I see the damage done already and I can't help but think that if only I had let Baron Barnett have his way none of this would have happened."

Awbrey patted Sophie's back. "No wonder you've been so cross, carrying such a burden. It is not your fault, Sophie."

"I have not been cross," Sophie said, pulling away.

"Very well," Awbrey said. She stood and felt her way back to her bed in the dark. "But it's not your fault. You don't control what the man does. If you had let him have his way with you he would have still done this. And then you would be sitting in Lethbridge hating yourself and watching him do all this."

Awbrey had almost fallen asleep when Sophie spoke. "Thank you, Awbrey."

Awbrey thought the words "you are welcome" but it was too much effort to actually say the words and she fell asleep.

The sun had not yet risen when Romke woke them with knocking on the door. Awbrey rubbed the sleep from her eyes as she stumbled to the door and opened it. Romke stepped inside and shut the door behind him. Sophie sat up on the bed, rubbing her eyes. When she saw Romke standing in the room she shook Gemma until the girl finally opened her eyes.

"The officials are questioning anyone coming up the river," Romke said. "I've sent Tucker back to the ship. He's going to stay with the captain. I am taking the wagon out before sunrise. Alone. Jaydin has agreed to take the form of a horse. I don't know if he can manage more than a pony but that will do. Sophie, you will ride Eddy's horse and Gemma will ride Jaydin. You will ride out of town to meet me."

"I get to ride Jaydin?" Gemma asked, sitting up.

"Awbrey, you and Eddy will walk through town. Stop and look at window displays. Be leisurely. They will come after me and the wagon. When they find nothing of interest they will go on their way. Sophie, go east out of town, then ride north on the outskirts." Romke looked at the girls. "Is everything clear?"

Awbrey yawned, trying to wake up. She nodded, looking longingly at the bed. Once she had fallen asleep the small bed had not been so bad and now she longed to crawl back under the blankets. Awbrey suddenly realized that she was only wearing her chemise. She almost dived under the blankets before realizing that Romke had already seen her and he was already opening the door to leave again.

Romke looked back. "Get out there the moment you are dressed. No dawdling."

Once the door shut, Sophie and Awbrey quickly dressed. Gemma had fallen asleep in her clothes and waited by the door, impatient to reach the stables. The idea of riding Jaydin in the shape of a pony was so exciting to her that the moment the other two girls were adequately covered Gemma opened the door and dashed down the hall.

The sun announced its pending arrival with a pink glow in the sky when they met in the stable yard. Romke drove the wagon out into the street with a curt wave of his hand. Jaydin had already shifted shapes by the time they arrived in the stable. He was indeed more a large pony than a horse but big enough for a girl Gemma's size to ride. Sophie put a halter on his head with a lead rope, spread a blanket over his back, and helped Gemma up on his back. Eddy led his horse up to Sophie, saddled and ready to go. The girls rode out of the stable at a leisurely walk.

"We have time for breakfast," Eddy said. "There is a shop up the street that opens at sunrise. A bakery actually. So Romke said."

"Really? Breakfast now?" Awbrey asked. A sense of dread settled over her.

"It's too early for shopping. We have to delay but not at the inn," Eddy said.

Awbrey walked beside Eddy out of the stable yard. They crossed the cobbled street and Eddy walked up to the building on the corner and opened the door for Awbrey. She looked up in surprise and stepped into the shop.

The shop was a small bakery with shelves of breads, pastries, and muffins in a glass case. One wall was lined with simple wood shelving and held baskets filled with breads of every shape, size, and color. Three small tables, just big enough for two people to sit at, were lined up against a large window facing the street for those who chose to eat their purchases on site. The smell hit Awbrey as soon as Eddy opened the door. Baked breads. Awbrey took a deep breath, then another.

The couple looked at the delicacies in the glass case. Awbrey felt her mouth water when she saw the beautiful treats behind the glass. It felt like forever since she had had a baked pastry. Most people came into the shop and left with a loaf or few of bread. Five people came and left with their purchases in the short time while

Eddy and Awbrey browsed. They decided on savory meat tarts.

Eddy guided Awbrey to a table in the corner then went back to the counter and purchased their breakfast. The table still allowed them to see the inn but they were not on full display to the street through the window. Awbrey had eaten half of her egg and sausage tart when a group of five men marched past the shop. They went into the inn. In a few minutes they rushed out of the inn. Horses were brought and they mounted and rode past the bakery at a gallop.

Once the men passed the window on their way to the inn Awbrey forgot about eating. Fear clogged her throat as she watched the men race down the street, knowing they were going in search of the wagon. The man leading and giving orders wore an owl on his chest. People continued to enter the bakery, make their purchase, and leave. A normal day for them.

"Susan was right," Eddy said. "We should have tried this bakery long ago."

"What?" Awbrey asked in confusion, tearing her wide-eyed gaze from the inn door where a man lingered.

"Not only is it actually closer, it is undoubtedly superior," Eddy said. "Don't you think so? How was your tart?"

"Very good," Awbrey muttered.

"I'm going to bring back some pastries," Eddy said. "You stomach will settle once the morning has passed. Would some tea help? We should have some tea."

An older gentleman at a nearby table chuckled. Awbrey's face burned. Eddy made it sound like he was suggesting that she was with child. Eddy did not wait for her to have a chance to respond, jumping to his feet and going up to the counter to buy an assortment of pastries. A man in a suit entered the shop and stood behind Eddy to wait his turn.

The uniformed man standing near the inn entrance walked across the way to the bakery. He entered the shop. Eddy looked up from selecting his pastries, nodding a greeting then went back to pointing out which pastries he wanted to clerk to add to the bag.

"You there," the official said to the shop clerk. "Did a large group come in or pass by? A group of young folk with one child?"

The clerk handed Eddy the package of pastries and took the coin. "Lots of people shop here, sir. That's why we are open," the clerk said.

The man waiting behind Eddy stepped up to the counter when Eddy turned and went back to the table. The man handed the clerk a list of items. The clerk immediately turned and began filling a basket with bread loaves and pastries, glancing repeatedly at the slip of paper to make sure he did not miss anything. More people came into the shop, some lining up behind the official and some looking at the displays to decide what they wanted.

"You there," the official snapped at the clerk. "I am not done with you."

"Oh, but Governer Rable's man is current in the queue. You're next," the busy clerk said over his shoulder.

"I am not here for any bloody pastries," the official snapped.

"Oh, then if you don't mind, could you step out of the queue?" the woman behind him asked. "I am scheduled to be at the Hammonds in under an hour."

The official stepped out of the way. There were seven people in the queue now and the clerk was busy trying to fill their orders as quickly as possible. The official was irritated but ready to give up when his gaze fell on Awbrey.

Caught staring, Awbrey quickly averted her gaze down to the food on her plate. The official strode to the table, looking down at Awbrey and Eddy but his focus was on Awbrey. "I have never seen you before," the official said to Awbrey. "Did you just arrive in town?"

"Leave be, Mort, the man sitting next them said. "They live in the area. Newlyweds. It's bad luck to pester a young woman in the family way."

"Friends of yours, Mister Henne?" the official asked more politely.

"No. But I tend to eavesdrop and they live in the area. This new law sure has people on edge. What nonsense. Scurrying about like there is some emergency," Mister Henne said.

The official relaxed even more. "Aye. That baron sure has everyone walking lightly."

Awbrey opened her mouth to ask if the baron himself was in Green Falls and Eddy kicked her shin under the table. Awbrey glared at Eddy but kept her thoughts to herself.

"The man in the owl sigil?" Mister Henne asked. "If he's here to enforce the king's new law why is he not wearing a stallion?"

The official, Mort, shrugged. "While he's here everyone is sure jumping though. Hopefully he don't stay too long."

With that Mort left the shop without giving Awbrey and Eddy another glance. Mister Henne finished his tea and also left the shop. Eddy stood and Awbrey followed. They walked north holding hands, in no hurry. Other people walked about also, some hurrying along to destinations and some sauntering in no hurry.

"It sure is an active town," Eddy said, looking around them.

"That was so embarrassing. Why did you make it sound like I am pregnant?" Awbrey asked.

"Your face turned green when that group of men rode past. It was the first thing I could think of to explain away your reaction. It worked, didn't it?"

"I guess," Awbrey said grudgingly.

"What will we name our first born child?" Eddy asked.

"Clovis," Awbrey said without hesitation. "Clovis Hans for a boy. A girl will be Lenane Bud."

Eddy threw back his head and laughed heartily. "It's a good think we're discussing this now. I have enough time to convince you on other names."

"What is wrong with Clovis?"

Eddy stopped in his tracks. "Wait. Wasn't Clovis your stuffed rabbit toy?"

"I loved that rabbit," Awbrey said with a smile.

For a while Awbrey almost forgot that they were hunted fugitives as they walked along the city center, looking at the stores and shops lining the street. Some shops had enticing window displays while some shops had more simple displays of their wares. Awbrey stopped in front of a window that had an anvil sitting on the windowsill inside and nothing else. It was not the anvil that caught her attention. It was that there was an anvil and only an anvil that caught her attention.

Eddy stared at the anvil on the other side of the window. "In the mood to buy an anvil?" he asked lightly.

"I've never had an anvil. I wonder what I could use it for?" Awbrey said. Eddy looked at her in surprise and Awbrey laughed. "The look on your face was priceless."

"I was dreading having to haul an anvil up the hill," Eddy said in his defense.

They continued walking, now pointing out items that were the least likely to interest the other. They were just two young people in love, enjoying each other's company. Eventually the stores thinned and they left the congested city center. The street was now lined with homes and other buildings. The grade of the street gradually grew steeper and Awbrey could feel the incline in her calves. As they walked past houses they discussed the merits and aspects of the houses compared to what they would like for their house when they married.

The sound of galloping shod hooves broke the relaxed mood they had been sharing. The same men who had ridden off after the wagon from the inn rode into sight at the top of the hill the couple was approaching. The mounted men were headed back to the city center in a very big hurry. Awbrey instantly averted her gaze.

"Don't look away," Eddy said when Awbrey turned her head away from the street. "That attracts more attention when you do the opposite of everyone else, opposite of what's natural. It's natural to watch a group of crazy men galloping through town."

So Awbrey looked up at the men riding down the center of the street. The man in the lead wearing a white snowy owl sigil on his chest looked angry. It was not easy to clearly see his face from that distance but she could see the anger. He clenched his teeth and stared straight ahead with a determined glare. As he passed Eddy and Awbrey he glanced down, making eye contact with Awbrey.

Images flowed. Awbrey sucked in her breath and dropped her gaze to her feet, overwhelmed by the impressions coming from the man. The whole incident happened in less than the blink of an eye. The riders continued on without Baron Barnett even really noticing Awbrey. If he had seen her he only saw another young person walking in Green Falls.

"He's magic," Awbrey said in surprise. She turned to Eddy. "He *is* magic. Why would he make being magic illegal when he's magic?"

Eddy watched the riders for a while longer. "So that's Baron Barnett? What is he doing in Green Falls? That's an odd coincidence. He must have been in Ava also. He followed the river. Like he knew we would be on the river." Eddy turned to Awbrey. "How do you know he's magic?"

"That crystal ball. He can't use it if he has no magic. He used it and that's why he's doing this. He saw something that he's afraid of. He's trying to change the future," Awbrey said. "Sophie. How could Sophie not know?" she muttered under her breath.

"What would bring him here himself?" Eddy asked frowning. "Why not send men to bring us back? Why come himself? Even if he knew where we would be heading, why could he not trust his men? Why did he feel he had to come himself?"

"He saw something. He is the only one who knows what he is looking for," Awbrey said.

Chapter Eleven

"If he found the crystal ball in the wagon he would not have left Romke behind," Eddy said, looking up the hill in the direction Romke had gone. He looked back at Awbrey. "He didn't find it did he? Isn't it the future you see? Did you see him using the crystal ball in the future?"

"Just impressions," Awbrey said. She shook her head and started walking again, briskly despite her complaining calves. "Just impressions. Whatever is ahead is because of what he saw in the past and he wants to change it."

"The old man was smart to split us up like this," Eddy said, walking beside her and picking up even more speed with his longer legs. "They were looking for a group. Because they were looking for a group they didn't even give us a second look." Eddy chuckled and shook his head. "Amazing. If I had not seen it for myself I would never have believed it. Because they were looking for something specific they did not notice anything else."

It was difficult to talk and maintain their hurried pace so they fell silent, concentrating on going as fast as possible without actually breaking into a run. As they walked up the hill the river became visible to their left. Awbrey stared at the churning white water filled with black boulders. The water vanished farther ahead. The falls. White spray filled the air where the river vanished.

Awbrey tripped on a tree root. She caught herself and managed to not fall. The rougher section of road required her attention and she had to stop staring at the river so that she could watch where she was walking. Eddy glided along beside her, his long legs striding smoothly without even any apparent effort.

Awbrey glanced over her shoulder. They were quite high above the town now, giving a clear view all the way down to the center of town. A commotion in the center of town caught her attention and Awbrey slowed. She stopped walking and turned to see what was happening. A crowd was gathering with men on horseback riding amongst the crowd. There were more than a dozen riders now.

"What are they doing?" Awbrey asked.

"Gathering a crowd, whatever it is," Eddy said.

He tilted his head as he watched the officials ride away and then return to the city center. A rider rode in their direction but stopped at a house halfway between them and the city center. The man went inside the house and came out carrying a child tucked under his arm. He jumped on his horse and galloped back to the city center. A woman ran out of the house after him, screaming, but he was already a good distance away.

Awbrey gathered up her skirt in her hand to free her legs and ran down to the house where the woman stood. Behind her Eddy swore then followed.

"My boy! My boy!" the woman screamed to the fleeing rider.

"What happened?" Awbrey asked.

The woman turned, just seeing them. "He took my son," the woman cried out in despair. She clutched Awbrey's hands and sobbed. "I have two more in the house so I can't leave them."

"What is your son's name?" Awbrey asked.

"Jarred. He took my Jarred," the woman said. She sagged where she stood. "He said the baron ordered it. The town is harboring magic users so the town will be punished."

"I will find Jarred," Awbrey promised.

"No," Eddy said. "I'm sorry but we can't," he said more gently to the woman. He turned back to Awbrey. "We can't. We have to go."

"But he's hurting children," Awbrey said.

"Hurting children?" the woman asked in horror.

"We don't know that he's hurting children," Eddy said. Awbrey stared at him, chin rising. "We don't know," Eddy insisted.

The woman ran back inside the house. Another uniformed rider appeared, stopping at another house further up the hill. He came out with a child in his arms. Jarred's mother returned to the door with an infant in her arms and a toddler stepping delicately beside her. The rider galloped past with a wailing girl bouncing on the saddle in front of him.

Awbrey picked up the toddler and pushed him at Eddy. "You'll have to carry him."

"It's Alison," the woman said, watching the rider pass. "She's the same age as my Jarred."

Eddy reluctantly took the child and followed Awbrey and Jarred's mother as they raced for the center of town where the crowd gathered. Baron Barnett was standing on a platform. He was yelling but the gathered crowd was too big to get close enough to hear.

"What is happening?" Jarred's mother asked a man standing next to them on the edge of the crowd.

"The baron there is saying that there's a ship on the dock and he's filling it with the children. He's going to send it up the falls," another man standing in front of them said.

Jarred's mother started screaming and pushed her way into the crowd. The infant in her arms wailed. The crowd parted enough to let the woman in and then closed up again, blocking Awbrey and Eddy from following.

Awbrey and Eddy stood on the edge of the crowd with the woman's child. The small boy Eddy held started squealing and squirming in Eddy's grip when his mother left his sight. Eddy bounced up and down trying to calm the boy. The child just squirmed even more.

As the news spread through the crowd the uproar rumbled as loud as the falls. The crowd grew agitated and surged closer to the platform. There were about twenty children standing or sitting on the platform next to the baron. Many were crying. Several huddled together in groups of two or three. Uniformed men surrounded them, stepping in and roughly pushing back any child who tried to break free.

Several uniformed riders used their horses to block people in the crowd from approaching the children. Some even had to kick people away. It was a noisy, chaotic mass of confusion and anger. Baron Barnett grabbed one of the children standing next to him on the platform and held the girl in the air. Whatever he said made the people nearest him back away but people who did not hear continued to push forward.

"He doesn't have enough men to hold back this crowd," Eddy said, shaking his head.

Even as he spoke, uniformed reinforcements arrived. The armed men pushed their way brutally through the crowd, knocking people down if they did not move. They reached the platform and formed a ring around the baron and the abducted children. The men on horseback pushed their way into the security of the circle, helping to enforce the barricade.

The people of Green Falls were not about to back off when their children were threatened. Though area had cleared around the baron the crowd did not disperse. In fact, the crowd of angry people grew. There was no sign of Jarred's mother in the crowd. Eddy pushed the toddler he held at Awbrey.

"Take him, Awbrey. Let me find his mother," Eddy said.

Awbrey took the child. He was heavier than he looked and she swung him onto her hip. Eddy pushed his way into the crowd. Awbrey stood on her tiptoes trying to see what was going on. The toddler stopped squirming but continued to cry, sad, heart breaking sobs. Awbrey patted him on the back soothingly but her attention was on spotting Eddy or the child's mother. The baron was still holding the child out at the end of his arm, the poor girl kicking the air and screaming.

It seemed to happen in slow motion. The young girl twisted her head and bit Baron Barnett's hand. Baron Barnett growled and flung the child away. The girl spun in the air like a rag doll, right at the packed and jostled horses. Then the girl stopped moving and hung in empty air. She just hung there. The crowd went dead silent.

"A magic user!" Baron Barnett screamed.

Baron Barnett swung his arm, probably a gesture meant to urge his men after the unknown magic user. Lightning streaked from his fingertips, striking a building across the street. Where the lightning struck a small explosion sent bricks and dust flying with a loud boom. Awbrey saw the shock on the man's face and knew that Eddy had done the little trick. Hopefully no one else guessed that the baron had not expected lightning to erupt from his fingers.

Awbrey twisted and turned through the mass of people standing in front of her, dodging when necessary to fight her way through the crowd to the small girl hanging in the air. Awbrey reached the girl and stepped directly under her. The girl slowly, gently dropped into Awbrey's free arm. The girl wrapped her arms around Awbrey's neck so tightly that Awbrey could barely breathe.

Baron Barnett's eyes grew wide when he saw Awbrey then narrowed in rage. "You!" he screamed. He raised his arm, likely to signal his men. Lightning flew from his fingertips once again. Several charred seagulls dropped from the sky onto the crowd, feathers smoking.

"Hey, Baron, we found our magic user," a voice yelled from the crowd. "You!"

The crowd surged forward again. Awbrey felt hands on her, guiding her out of the crowd. Soft hands. Hard hands. Firm hands. Small hands. The way opened before her and many hands steadied her and pushed her along out of danger.

Awbrey glanced over her shoulder, looking for Eddy. The barrier of armed men had been broken and a trail of children followed her out to the edge of the crowd. The little ones too scared to walk themselves were being handed from person to person. Awbrey reached the edge of the crowd and was immediately swarmed by parents rushing to gather their children.

Mothers rushed toward her. Children ran past her to fathers and mothers. Uncles and neighbors called out children's names as they saw them exiting the crowd. A grateful father snatched the girl out of Awbrey's arms, tears running down his face. A woman joined him, embracing them both.

Awbrey breathed in relief. The girl had been heavy as well as choking her the whole way through the ordeal. Suddenly the parents and relatives of the released children were all hugging her and thanking her and it was difficult to breathe again. Awbrey spotted Romke making his way to her and she carefully pulled away from the grateful crowd of people suffocating her.

"Yes, he was hurting children," Romke said in greeting. "But don't think this will stop him."

"They have to arrest him as a magic user," Awbrey said. "Right? His own men have to arrest him now." The toddler on her hip was squirming and Awbrey shifted him higher on her hip to keep him from falling.

Romke tilted his head slightly and did a small shake of his head. "Not necessarily," he said slowly, looking down as he considered the odds that Baron Barnett's men would actually arrest him.

Baron Barnett had mounted a horse and kicked the horse to plunge right through the crowd, pushing his way through without caring who got trampled in the process. The horse threw its head back, shaking its head against the reins biting into its soft mouth but kept moving forward against the spurs dug into its sides. Several people were knocked off their feet and the crowd parted reluctantly, slowly in the baron's path.

Awbrey twisted out of the way even as Romke grabbed her arm and pulled her back, trying to move her out of the way of the frightened, charging horse. Awbrey fell to one knee but Romke pulled her back to her feet. Baron Barnett's attention was on Awbrey, his gaze locked on her. He did not even notice the people he was knocking out of the way. The people making up the crowd were reaching their limit.

A man grabbed for the horse's reins while several people grabbed the baron's legs and tried to drag him off the horse. The horse turned in a circle around the man holding his reins. Baron Barnett managed to stay on the horse, kicking one man right in the face and slashing at the rest with a riding crop. The baron's men were fighting their way to his side, pushing away the people who were trying to pull Baron Barnett off his horse.

Baron gestured at Awbrey. "Take her," he yelled.

The uniformed men surrounded Awbrey, blocking Romke with their horses. One man pulled the child from her grip and another lifted her onto his horse in front of him. Awbrey was more concerned at first with the boy she had been holding and twisted in the man's grasp, trying to see where the child had gone. The man holding her tightened his arm around her waist to keep her from slipping off the saddle.

Baron Barnett led the way away from the crowd and galloped up the street. The uniformed men raced after him. Now Awbrey feared for herself as the rider holding her kicked his horse into a gallop after the baron. Awbrey twisted and kicked despite the speed of the galloping horse she sat on. Fear gave her energy and strength but the iron grip holding her did not falter.

Awbrey expected help to set her free at any minute and stopped struggling. Surely Eddy would free her from this man's grip. Why did Jaydin not turn into a bear or wolf and spring into the path of the horse? Someone could help her. Sophie could simply tell the horse to stop.

Nothing stopped the riders as they galloped through the streets, twisting and turning through the town. The group of men rode unchallenged up to an inn, where they slowed as they rode into the inn's stable yard. The soldier holding Awbrey released her into the arms of another uniformed soldier. He was tall and solidly built with an expressionless face and blonde hair.

Baron Barnett slid off his horse and strode through the inn's entrance without even a glance behind him. Awbrey looked up at the sign hanging over the door. A rock with churning white river water flowing over it was painted on the sign above the name, The Whitewater Inn. The uniformed man holding her lowered her until her feet touched the ground, then gripped her arm tightly and pulled her towards the inn's entrance.

The main floor was a tavern with smoke-stained low beam ceiling. Baron Barnett ran up the wide staircase to the second floor and entered a private room at the rear of the inn, his men following closely at his heels, including the man keeping a firm grip on Awbrey. Her escort pulled her into the room behind the baron.

A large window provided a breath-sucking view of the river below. A large table with eight chairs placed around the table took up most of the room. Awbrey could see the river continue from the drop of the falls and emerge beyond the white spray floating over the falls through the window. He had meant to send children in a ship over that? If he did, he meant them all to die.

The uniformed man escorting Awbrey released her and stepped back. Four more men had entered the room with the baron but the rest remained in the hall. The door was shut from without.

The baron was livid with rage. He paced in front of the window for several minutes, oblivious to the view. He was an average looking man. Though he had a slightly bulbous nose and thick, black eyebrows, he was not at all what Awbrey would have expected from Sophie's description of him. Awbrey had expected to see a monster, yet the baron was so ordinary looking that he was almost nondescript. Average height, average build, and average face. The baron's brown hair was cut short and slightly receding but he was not so old as she had imagined either.

Awbrey's knees trembled as she waited. The adrenaline running through her for so long was receding and the shock of the recent events hit her body suddenly. Awbrey moved to a chair near her to sit but the uniformed man who had escorted her into the room pulled her back, shaking his head at her.

The movement caught the baron's attention and he stopped pacing, facing Awbrey. There was a harshness to his face because of his mood. He looked close to an age as her parents now that she faced him straight on. Closer, she could see the fine lines on his face, the touch of gray at his temples. Surely too old to be pestering girls Sophie's age.

"You," Baron Barnett said. "I have seen you before."

Awbrey started to shake her head no then remembered that he had ridden past her as she and Eddy walked out of town. "You passed us as we were walking this morning."

Baron Barnett frowned. "No. I have seen you before today. Who are you?"

"I have never seen you before today," Awbrey said. Her upper lip tingled and she swayed slightly.

"Who are you?" Baron asked, stepping closer to her.

He smelled like Romke's stinky sausages and body odor. Awbrey clamped her mouth shut and took a step back, into the solid, unmoving body of the uniformed man who continued to stand guard over her. The baron was scaring her. Even without his reputation, in person he was intimidating, especially with his angry face too close to her face. Baron Barnett glared at her, eyes narrowing.

"My name is Awbrey," Awbrey said softly.

"But who are you?"

"I don't understand," Awbrey said, a touch of fear making her voice quiver.

A knock on the door pulled Baron Barnett's attention away from Awbrey. He walked to the door and opened it, stepping out into the hall to talk to someone.

"You would do well to cooperate," her guard said.

"But I don't understand what he wants," Awbrey said, turning to face the man behind her.

"Just tell him who you are."

"I did. I am Awbrey. Just Awbrey."

The guard looked down at her. His face softened and he shook his head in sympathy for the young girl who was clearly confused. The man did not say anything more. He put a hand on her shoulder and turned her so that she was facing the window again.

The door opened and Baron Barnett returned to the room. He ignored Awbrey. He walked to the window and stared out at the river for several minutes. When he turned to Awbrey he was calmer than he had been when they first entered the room.

"That was quite the trick, making it look like I was throwing magic. There's some rumbling about it now but it will pass. Was it you? Or someone in your little party?" Baron asked in a cold voice.

"I saw that. It surprised me to learn that you are a magic user when you are the one who made it illegal," Awbrey said.

The baron struck Awbrey in the face with the back of his hand. The force of the blow unbalanced her. She almost fell over but her guard grabbed her shoulders and held her upright. Awbrey sobbed in pain and fear, reaching up to gingerly touch her cheek where the baron hit her.

It was the first time in her life that Awbrey had been struck by a person. The pain went deeper than the physical blow. Humiliation struck her as hard as the baron's hand. She was just as shocked at how embarrassed, how exposed she felt being struck. Awbrey wanted to fight back, to stand up against him, but the truth was that he terrified her.

"The king outlawed magic users, not me," Baron Barnett snarled.

Awbrey leaned back against her guard, finding some comfort in his solid form. Tears ran down her face and her nose was dripping now.

"Tell me who you are," Baron Barnett said.

Awbrey kept her mouth shut. She had already told him who she was and he did not like it. There seemed to be no right answer. The baron raised his fist and Awbrey closed her eyes, cringing as she waited for the blow to land. Anticipation was almost as bad as the actual strike. No punch landed and after a few minutes passed Awbrey opened one eye.

Baron Barnett stood glaring at her but he had lowered his fist. "I've seen you. In the ball."

The ball. It took a second before Awbrey realized that he meant the crystal ball that Romke had hidden in the wagon. It felt peculiar to think that this man, advisor to the king, the man who had most of the country gripped in fear, knew her face from gazing into a crystal ball. Awbrey was curious to know what he had seen within that mysterious crystal ball but she was not about to ask him. Was it just impressions like she saw? Or could he manipulate the ball to show what he wanted? Specific events?

Another knock on the door interrupted the baron. One of baron's men stuck his head around the partially opened door. "Sir, you should see this," the man said.

"Everyone out," the baron said, gesturing to his men. He looked at Awbrey. "When I return you will answer my questions." He looked up at her guard behind her. "Convince her."

The other men left with the baron, leaving Awbrey alone with her guard. Awbrey tried again to sit on a chair and the man moved the chair away from her before she could sit. Awbrey walked to the next chair and put her hand on it, leaning her weight on her arm. The guard did not seem to have a problem with her using the chair to support her and let her be.

Awbrey studied the man. He looked older than Eddy but not by that many years. He did not have a kind face but neither did he have an unkind face. The guard was a soldier, sculpted into a man who obeyed orders and kept his feelings out of the mix.

"Perhaps I could have something to drink," Awbrey said.

The man shook his head. "Not yet."

Awbrey walked to the window and looked out at the river. Spray from the water beating against the rocks hung over the river so she could not see how far the drop actually was. At least the children were safe. Thinking about what Baron Barnett had planned for the children stiffened her spine. Then she realized what he would be willing do to her if he was willing to harm innocent children just to make a point and some of her resolve slipped away.

"I need something to drink," Awbrey said, turning to her guard. "If I pass out from thirst I won't be talking much."

"You aren't going to pass out after an hour of no water," the man said.

"I've been walking all morning. I ran all the way to the city center from the top of the hill," Awbrey said. Her stomach growled loudly. "I am not asking for food. Just water."

The guard opened the door and talked to one of the men in the hall. He waited at the door, keeping an eye on Awbrey. In a few minutes a man in the hall handed her guard a tray with a pitcher of water and two glasses and shut the door as the guard carried the tray to the table. When he set the tray on the table Awbrey saw that there was also a plate with two buns, several slabs of cold roast beef, grapes, cheese, and carrots.

"Oh, thank you," Awbrey said politely when she saw the tray's contents.

Awbrey poured a glass of water and drank the whole thing down. The food looked and smelled very good but Awbrey had not been invited to eat so she poured another glass of water and went to stand in front of the window again as she drank the second glassful of water more leisurely.

The guard piled roast beef on the buns and poured mustard from a small bowl onto the meat. "Eat," he said, shoving a bun into her hand.

Mustard dripped onto Awbrey's fingers when she bit into the meat stuffed bun. She set the glass on the table and used both hands to eat, standing next to the table. Awbrey closed her eyes. She had never tasted food so delicious.

"You may sit," the guard said.

Awbrey sank gratefully onto the chair nearest her. The guard ate the second meat filled bun in only a few bites. "You're just a little girl," he muttered. "The law holds to anyone who aids magic users though."

"Those children were not breaking any laws," Awbrey said between bites.

"No," the man said.

"How can you punish children for no reason?" Awbrey asked.

The guard stared at her, taking some time to answer. "I follow orders. I have no choice."

"Everyone has a choice," Awbrey said.

The guard laughed. "Youth. I forget how simple it seems to the young."

"It's a stupid law and those children had nothing to do with it. I just about jumped out of my shoes when the baron started throwing lightning. Shouldn't you arrest him for being a magic user? Aren't those your orders?" Awbrey asked.

The man did not say anything but looked thoughtful as he helped Awbrey clean the food off the plate. Though Awbrey knew that Eddy must have had a hand in the baron's display of magic, it did not matter. Baron Barnett was magic and Eddy had just given up the baron's secret in a visible, public display.

When the food was gone the guard set the water pitcher on the table and carried the tray to the door. He remained in the doorway for several minutes, talking to the men in the hall. Awbrey could only hear a spattering of words. Example. Girl. The new law. Baron angry. Arrogant people. Town had no respect for the king's laws. Crush them.

The sound of pebbles hitting the window glass caught Awbrey's attention. It came again, a soft rattle of pebbles hitting the glass and rolling down the side of the building. Eddy! Awbrey jumped to her feet then composed herself and casually went to the window. Eddy stood on the grass below the window. Awbrey kissed her fingertips and put her fingers on the window. When he saw Awbrey he looked down and said something. Romke and Gemma stepped into view next to Eddy.

Her guard had shut the door but still stood near the door, head down in thought. Awbrey stepped back in surprise when the glass of the window shimmered and vanished. Tentatively Awbrey stuck her hand out and through the window opening. The glass was gone. She jerked her hand back in surprise.

"Jump," Romke called up to her.

Awbrey looked down at him in shock. Jump? It was a long way down. Eddy held up his arms like he was going to catch her. Awbrey glanced over her shoulder at the guard, who was still too absorbed in his own thoughts to notice that the glass in the window was no longer there. He glanced at her, frowned, and looked away again. Whatever he had been discussing with his fellow uniformed men had clearly unsettled him.

Even if Eddy managed to catch her, she still had to get up and out the window before the guard noticed. Awbrey took a deep breath, put her foot on the windowsill and dived head first out the window. Behind her she could hear the guard's surprised swearing. The air actually felt thick under her body as she slowly fell down. Romke stepped forward and Awbrey landed in his arms.

Awbrey glanced up at the window above them as Romke set her on her feet. The guard slapped his palm against the glass. The window was back in place. The guard did not stay long at the window and Awbrey imagined him running out of the room to sound the alarm that she had escaped.

"Hurry," Romke urged. They ran, Eddy taking the lead. They ran through yards, between bushes, past startled dogs. It felt that the whole way was uphill as well. It did not take long before a shout went up behind them.

"Now," Romke said to Gemma.

The girl began to hum then sing softly. Awbrey's scalp itched. Whatever the girl was doing, it felt like bugs were crawling all over her. Awbrey rubbed her arm. Romke nodded as he looked at Awbrey then guided them to the street. Eddy and Gemma followed, Gemma singing nonstop softly. Eddy held Gemma's hand.

"They'll see us," Awbrey said in alarm when Romke proceeded to walk up the street out of town in full view.

Metal horse shoes rang out on the cobblestoned street behind them, coming closer and closer. Awbrey walked with her head down, staring at the ground in front of her feet. Awbrey did not understand how they could so calmly walk along the side of the road. The trick of trying to blend in had worked once but would not work now that she had been identified.

Romke placed his hand on her arm and held her tightly. If he had not been holding her Awbrey would have run away to find someplace to hide. She could feel their eyes on her back. They were going to catch her again and this time they would take Eddy, Gemma, and Romke as well.

The baron had already been angry and filled with hate for her. He would be even more livid with rage that she had attempted to escape. Awbrey's heart raced. Awbrey tried to pull free of Romke's grip. She wanted to run. She wanted to run and not walk placidly along the road in plain sight.

"Trust me, Awbrey," Eddy said under his breath.

"Do something," Awbrey said in panic. "You can do something, Eddy. Do something. They are almost on us."

Chapter Twelve

Romke kept a firm grip on Awbrey's arm when she tried again to pull free so that she could run. "Walk slowly," he said.

"No. We must run," Awbrey said.

"Look at me, Awbrey," Eddy said.

Awbrey looked up at Eddy. He looked older, heavier. Only his eyes were Eddy's eyes. Awbrey looked at Romke, directly at Romke. He appeared to be even shorter with a bald head and a golden cast to his skin. Gemma still looked like Gemma, a girl singing a song about a carnival.

The riders crested the hill, slowed only slightly, giving the foursome a glance as they rode past then kicked their horses into a gallop again. Awbrey stared in shock. Her blonde guard was with them and he had looked right at her with no sign of recognition.

Uniformed men ran out into the street from the same location they had emerged onto the street. They looked up and down the street before splitting and continuing the search. One of the men ran right past them in the same direction the riders had gone.

"Keep it up, girl," Romke said when Gemma's voice faltered. "We're almost there."

Gemma straightened her shoulders and continued to sing. Eddy kept a firm grip on the young girl's hand, watching where they walked and guiding her around anything that would make her trip so that she could concentrate on singing.

They followed Romke as he left the road into the trees lining the road. After a few minutes they stepped out of the trees into a small clearing. The wagon waited in the clearing. Eddy's horse was tied to the back corner of the wagon. Sophie and Jaydin were sitting on the ground next to the wagon. They jumped to their feet when they saw Romke, searching the group in concern until they spotted Gemma. Jaydin opened the wagon door. Everyone piled into the wagon without delay.

Romke wasted no time. The wagon was moving by the time Jaydin shut the door. Once they were within the cover of the wagon Gemma stopped singing, panting from the effort it took to sing so long and while hurrying up a hill. Jaydin and Sophie settled onto the sofa on the left while Awbrey and Eddy sat on the right sofa. Gemma plopped down on the floor between the sofas. Awbrey watched Eddy return to himself.

"What did I look like?" Awbrey asked.

"An old grandmother," Sophie said with an angry chuckle.

"It worked," Eddy said quickly.

"Oh, I don't care if I looked like an old hag," Awbrey said. "Thank you, Gemma."

Though Awbrey felt relieved to be rescued she did not feel safe yet. Fear twisted her stomach in knots. Eddy understood. He sat next to her and held her close.

"We were almost free of this town. Romke's plan worked. If you hadn't gone back we would not have had to go through this elaborate rescue," Sophie said. Her voice was hard and angry. "I think I lost seven years of my life, afraid Baron Barnett would step into that clearing before you did."

"There were children," Eddy said.

"I'm sorry," Awbrey said. "To all of you. I put you in danger. But he was hurting children." Awbrey met Sophie's angry stare. "He is a bad man. He needs to be stopped."

"Do you think those townspeople were going to meekly let the baron hurt their children?" Sophie asked, leaning forward.

"She had to do something," Jaydin said.

Sophie turned her head and glared so fiercely at Jaydin that he leaned away from her, shoulders hunching. "We were almost free," Sophie said. "They didn't even know we were here until you stuck your nose in where it wasn't needed."

"They knew we were here," Eddy argued. "A small delay and we're on our way again. Let it rest, Sophie."

"How could she know that these townspeople would stand up to Baron Barnett? Remember Ava, Sophie" Jaydin said.

"How can I forget Ava?" Sophie snapped. "That is what I am afraid of."

Sophie settled back against the sofa but though she stopped

talking the anger poured off her like a physical wave. She glared at Awbrey as the wagon swayed and rocked its way along. It did not feel like Romke had pulled onto the road yet. The wagon protested the terrain he was driving it over.

Awbrey experienced a turmoil of emotion. Her face throbbed where Baron Barnett had struck her. The relief at being rescued reminded her of how serious the situation at the inn had been. Baron Barnett had planned on hurting her. She was not sure if she should feel sorry for her guard or not. Awbrey had no doubt that he would be in trouble for letting her escape. She hoped that he was not punished too severely. It did not enter her head that he had helped hold her prisoner. The man had given her water and food.

"It isn't fair," Awbrey muttered. "It just isn't fair. We did nothing wrong. I know that I've done nothing wrong. Yet he's driven us from our homes, our lives. We run, afraid. Yet for what?"

"No, it isn't fair," Eddy said. "Life isn't fair."

"We run to stay alive," Jaydin said at the same time.

"It isn't about fairness," Sophie said. "When will you get that through your thick head? It is about the person who wants something getting his own way. In this case it's the baron. It's never about fairness. Fairness is a fairy tale."

"Sophie," Eddy started to say.

"No, Eddy. She's right," Awbrey said. "I held onto that idea because I could not imagine someone being so callous to not care about who he hurt. Now that I've met the baron I can see it. All he cares about is getting his way, destroying anything getting in his way."

"Finally," Sophie muttered.

"You of all people should know that it is not my fault what the baron does, Sophie," Awbrey said in a cold voice. Sophie stared at Awbrey for a moment then looked away.

Awbrey's gaze drifted to the hidden compartment behind Sophie's feet. If the baron could use the crystal ball hidden there, Awbrey wondered if she could use it. Yet what good would it do to see the future? The snatches she glimpsed never did her or anyone any good.

The wagon rattled to a halt. Only for a moment. The wagon rocked and swayed as it started forward again, throwing everyone sideways. The wagon straightened and hit a bump before gaining speed again. Gemma crawled up on the sofa with Eddy and Awbrey.

Jaydin stared out the window above Awbrey's head. "We turned. Why is he heading back?"

Even as he asked the wagon slowed then stopped. The back door opened. Eddy untangled himself from Awbrey's arms and stepped out the door. As he stepped through the doorway an arm reached out, holding a knife. The blade slashed across Eddy's throat. Eddy crumpled like a mannequin having its threads snipped, falling out of sight.

Awbrey stared in disbelief for a heartbeat. Awbrey screamed Eddy's name as she leaped up from the sofa, evading Jaydin's hands as he tried to stop her. Awbrey dived out of the wagon, landing next to Eddy. She dropped to her knees beside him.

Blood poured from his neck. Too much blood. Awbrey took her hands in hers, oblivious to the uniformed men around her. Only Eddy existed. Except Eddy was dying.

"Help him!" Awbrey screamed. "Help him! Someone help him! Gemma! Gemma! Sing! Help him!"

Gemma cautiously stuck her head out the doorway, looking around before dropping to the ground next to Awbrey and Eddy. The girl put her hand on Eddy's chest, being careful to avoid the blood soaked up by his shirt. Awbrey felt a cold chill travel from Eddy's hands to her hands. The coldness spread up her arms and across her body.

"I'm sorry, Awbrey," Gemma said in a low voice. "It is too late." The girl's chin quivered.

"No!" Awbrey screamed at the girl. Gemma shrank back away from Awbrey, eyes wide. "He can't die. He is my Eddy. He can't die. No! No! No!"

Jaydin burst out of the wagon in the form of a wolf. His dive carried him over Eddy's form right in front of the two girls kneeling next to Eddy's body. The wolf ran only a few yards before the first arrow struck him in the side. Four more arrows struck him within seconds of the first arrow. The wolf collapsed and did not move.

Awbrey wrapped her arms around Eddy's shoulders and tried to lift him up. "Wake up. Wake up."

Gemma began to hum. Her eyes were wide and full of terror as she stared at the wolf body pierced with arrows then back to Eddy with his neck cut open and drenched with blood. The girl slowly rose from her knees to her feet as she hummed. Awbrey shivered as a vibration passed over her body. Gemma opened her mouth to sing and an arrow shaft flew past Awbrey with a whining sound straight into the younger girl's throat with a thunk when it struck her spine.

Awbrey stared up at the girl with the arrow shaft sticking out of her throat. The arrow was only inches from Awbrey's face. Gemma stood frozen for a moment, eyes wide and mouth open. The light in her eyes faded away. Then Gemma fell down.

Awbrey's scream was trapped within her. Her mouth opened and she raised her face to the sky but no sound escaped. Great sobs shook her small frame but she no longer made a sound.

Awbrey dropped her head onto her chest and sobbed. Losing her Eddy was so painful that she thought her heart would burst from the pain. Yet seeing Jaydin then young Gemma killed in front of her eyes pushed her over the edge beyond pain. She was a frozen statue of pain. Awbrey found it difficult to breath.

One of the uniformed men stepped over the two bodies into the wagon. He came out of the wagon dragging Sophie out by her hair. The man pushed Sophie down on the ground a few yards past Eddy and Gemma's bodies. Baron Barnett had been sitting on horseback watching the whole thing only a few yards away. Awbrey had not even noticed that he was there until he dismounted and stood over

Sophie.

"You will return with me to Lethbridge," Baron Barnett said to Sophie. The frail, blonde girl nodded, gaze locked on his feet.

Awbrey wrapped her fingers through Eddy's fingers and used her free hand to close his eyes. Blood drenched the front of her dress as well as her arms. The blood was now cold and sticky. The smell of earth and sun-warmed grasses blended with the smell of blood and death. Awbrey was dead inside. Life had no meaning without Eddy. Fresh sobs wracked her body.

"Burn the wagon. Bring the two girls," the baron barked out to his men as he mounted his horse.

"The bodies?" one of the men asked.

"Toss them in the wagon before you fire it," Baron Barnett said.

Baron Barnett sat on his horse, watching his men as they obeyed his orders. Awbrey's guard from the inn tried to pull Awbrey from Eddy's body. Awbrey still clasped Eddy's hand and in death Eddy's fingers gripped Awbrey's fingers tightly. The guard pried Eddy's fingers from her fingers and pulled her away. Two uniformed men picked up Eddy and tossed him into the wagon without care. Awbrey moaned. Gemma's small limp form was casually tossed in after him.

Awbrey felt like life left her when the uniformed men casually tossed Eddy's body into the back of the wagon and he vanished from her sight. She sagged against her escort, unable to stand on weak legs. Another man helped her guard half carry, half drag her to a horse. Her guard mounted the horse while the other man held her upright.

The guard leaned over and pulled her up onto the horse in front of him. Awbrey did not resist. Nothing mattered with Eddy gone. She slumped sideways on the horse and her guard wrapped his arm around her waist to hold her upright.

Awbrey leaned against the man's chest, hearing his heart beat against her ear. She would never hear Eddy's heart beat again. Fresh tears poured from her eyes, drenching her face. Her Eddy was dead. Jaydin and Gemma were dead. Romke must be dead or he would have done something by now. Only Sophie remained alive. And herself, Awbrey realized. She was still alive though she had died inside.

"Why am I still alive?" Awbrey asked as the man guided his horse away from the wagon.

"Our baron has plans for you," the man said.

Awbrey stared at the wagon as the horse walked away. She could see Romke's body slumped on the driver's seat. They had filled him with arrows as well then pushed him out of the way to take control of the horses. Several uniformed men were unharnessing the horses, leading them to safety away from the wagon before they set it on fire.

Awbrey felt too numb to feel fear. Fear was an emotion. She felt nothing. Perhaps she should feel fear. What she felt was numb and cold to her very core. Awbrey sobbed. Great, wracking sobs overtook her, sobs that stole the air from her lungs and made her upper lip tingle. She sobbed onto the chest of a soldier whose name she did not know while his heart beat steadily beneath her cheek, knowing that she would never hear Eddy's heart beat again.

They returned to the Whitewater Inn. The guard carried Awbrey to a room and gently laid her on the bed. He left her there. Awbrey curled into a ball on the bed and cried for hours without moving. The room slowly darkened as the day passed.

When the door opened and Sophie entered the room Awbrey did not move. She had no tears left to cry but she also had no energy, no will left to move a muscle. A servant followed Sophie into the room with a tray. Sophie waited near the door until the servant set down the tray and left the room.

"Awbrey," Sophie said, hurrying to the bed the second the door clicked shut.

Awbrey struggled to rouse herself, to find some reason, any reason to move an arm, a leg. It was so much effort. Awbrey did not care about making any effort. Awbrey did not move or respond to Sophie.

Sophie sat on the edge of the bed, hugging herself. "He did not touch me, thankfully."

Awbrey stared at Sophie but her eyes were vacant. Sophie frowned, leaning over Awbrey to look more closely at the girl. Awbrey's eyes were red and puffy from hours of crying. Dried snot caked her nose. Her hair was a wild tangle.

"I am sorry about Eddy," Sophie said. "And Gemma and

Jaydin."

Awbrey blinked. Awbrey frowned, looking at Sophie as if just realizing that she was there in the room, sitting next to her on the bed. Awbrey forced herself to sit up.

"And Romke," she whispered in a voice gone hoarse from so many hours of crying.

"Oh, dear," Sophie said, eyes watering.

"Eddy is dead," Awbrey whispered. "My Eddy is dead. They killed little Gemma as well. Just a little girl. Gemma was just a little girl who liked to sing and they killed her."

"Her singing was, well, yes she was just a little girl," Sophie said.

"And Jaydin. They killed Jaydin. You know, the only time I saw him in a different form was when he tried to help someone. The last time I guess it was himself he tried to help. He never hurt anyone. He did not have a mean bone in his body," Awbrey said. She choked on her next words. "And Romke. Strong Romke who took us under his wing because he wanted to save us. Our wonderful Uncle Romke is dead. He treated us like we were his own children."

"I didn't think anything could kill Romke," Sophie said.

Some of the anguish subsided as Awbrey talked. A spark of herself filled her eyes. She sat up straighter instead of hunched over. Awbrey became more aware of her surroundings. Sophie's casual demeanor rankled her nerves into life.

"Don't you care?" Awbrey asked, noticing the other girl's clear eyes and seeming indifference.

"Care? Of course I care," Sophie said.

"You don't look like you care," Awbrey said harshly.

Sophie pulled back. "Just because I am not wallowing in self-pity does not mean I don't care."

"Self-pity? They are dead. Dead!" Awbrey said, voice rising.

"And we are not," Sophie said, jumping to her feet. She walked to the tray the servant had brought in with her and uncovered one of the plates. "Maybe you will feel better after you have eaten."

The smell of food did not appeal to Awbrey. "Why not? Why were we spared?" Awbrey asked. "You are as magic as Jaydin."

"Eat, Awbrey," Sophie said, shoving a plate at her.

Awbrey ignored the plate so Sophie put it on Awbrey's lap. That was when Sophie noticed the blood covering Awbrey. It was mostly on her dress but it was also caked on her arms. The sight of the dried blood effected Sophie and she jerked her hand back, almost spilling the contents of the plate into Awbrey's lap. Tears filled her eyes but none fell.

"I know Baron Barnett's plans for me. I do not know his plans for you," Sophie said, backing away from the bed.

"Indeed," Awbrey said.

Sophie gasped at that simple word. It was like Romke was in the room for a moment. Awbrey did not even realize that she had used Romke's favorite word. Sophie collected herself and took a deep breath.

"Maybe he believes the same as you, that you are not magic. But you are. I can feel the magic in you," Sophie said.

"Is that what you talked to him about? That I am magic?" Awbrey asked.

Sophie's cheeks flushed and she turned her head. "Maybe if you can see the future you can change the future."

"It's the past I want to change," Awbrey said. She set the plate to her side on the bed. "What are the baron's plans for you, Sophie?"

"He has agreed that the best solution is to marry me," Sophie said.

Awbrey stared at the girl in surprise. "You want to marry him?"

"Want? No. But marriage is better than a mistress. Once his wife is gone, he--"

"Gone? Do you mean he intends to kill his wife to marry you?" Awbrey asked, cutting Sophie off before she could finish her sentence.

Sophie frowned. "I am sure he won't kill her. She'll just go away."

"As you'll just go away when something better comes along?" Awbrey asked. "I didn't think you were naïve, Sophie."

"It is the only way," Sophie said, approaching the bed again. "Don't you understand? It is the only way I have out. The only way to survive."

"Survive?" Awbrey mouthed the word. A memory tugged at the back of her mind. She looked up at Sophie. "You knew. You knew that the baron is magic yet you never said anything."

"What?" Sophie said, frowning.

"You can sense magic. You spent weeks in his company in Lethbridge. You had to know that he is magic. Why did you never say anything?"

Sophie shrugged. "It wasn't relevant."

"Not relevant?" Awbrey asked.

"Eat, Awbrey," Sophie said, gesturing at the plate of food sitting next to Awbrey on the bed.

Awbrey pushed the plate farther away from her. "I cannot believe you would marry that man after what he has done. Who he is."

"It is the only option for me," Sophie said. "I told you before that I wouldn't have any choice in who I married. At least he…"

The door of the room opened without even a warning knock, interrupting Sophie. A uniformed man stepped through the door, gaze on Awbrey. "He wants to see you, girl."

Chapter Thirteen

Awbrey stared up at the soldier looking at her. A knot twisted her stomach. Very slowly she got off the bed and walked across the room to the door and out into the hall. Two more soldiers waited in the hall. Awbrey demurely followed them though her legs trembled. Her blonde guard was not one of the three.

The soldiers led her out of the inn instead of to the private room where Baron had talked to her before. Awbrey's body shook as well as her legs now. She trembled so much that she almost fell. One of the soldiers stepped up next to her and took her arm. He held her up when she sagged again. Saddled horses were waiting and Awbrey was led to one of the horses.

The soldier bent down and grabbed her foot, lifting her up to the saddle. Awbrey swung her other leg over the horse's back and settled into the saddle. The horse she rode did not have a bridle with reins. Instead it had a halter with a lead rope. The rest of the men mounted their horses. One of the men held the lead rope of her horse and led her horse out of the stable yard. They rode downhill to the city center.

The baron stood on the same platform he had used as a stage

earlier that day. A hanging platform had been constructed next to the platform. A crowd of townspeople had gathered again, not certain what was happening. More people were walking toward the platform from different directions. A low murmur spread through the crowd as Awbrey was led through them to the platform. Baron Barnett waited for her there.

"It is the king's law that magic users are wanted criminals," the baron shouted to the crowd.

A uniformed man pulled Awbrey from the horse and dragged her roughly up onto the hanging platform though she did not protest or resist in any way. Her heart raced. Her legs trembled. Awbrey tried to stand straight and tall but her whole body started shaking.

"This girl is a magic user. Associated with magic users," the baron yelled, gesturing at Awbrey.

"You are going to kill that girl? Without even a trial?" a man wearing a white apron over his clothes asked, stepping out of the crowd. "What has she done to earn a hanging?"

"I told you. She is a magic user," Baron Barnett yelled.

"That's the girl who saved my Mary," a woman called out.

"Aye. She saved our children this day. From you!"

"Seems like you are determined to do some killing of innocents this day," a man said.

Awbrey recognized the man speaking from the coffee shop that morning. Had it only been just that morning? It seemed ages ago that Eddy and she had walked along the store fronts, looking at the window displays. Eddy was dead. Awbrey had no more tears to shed. The numbness that had settled over her in the clearing when she realized that Eddy was really dead settled over her again.

"I can still toss your brats into a boat and send them on a wild ride down the falls," Baron Barnett yelled, spittle flying from his mouth.

"I think the king should decide," coffee shop man said. "Who are you to come into our town and threaten innocent children over a law no one even heard of until you brought it to us a few days ago? You seem mighty eager to kill children who have done no wrong."

The crowd mumbled in agreement. Awbrey caught a few words. Trial. Extreme. Over eager. Rash. King. Most of the mumbling was a blur. She stared out into the crowd, seeing faces that were angry and confused and determined. Many faces looked sympathetic and concerned as well.

Baron Barnett made a gesture and a soldier put an arrow in coffee shop man's chest. "You seem eager to die," the baron yelled at the man's collapsed form below him.

Awbrey gasped in disbelief as she saw the man struck down in front of her. Every time she thought she could feel nothing more she felt more pain. Great sorrow filled her that the man had stood up for her, more than once, and now lay dead at her feet. It was not right that a good man died at the baron's whim simply for standing up to him.

The crowd's muttering grew to a roar. The uniformed men

lining the platforms stood firm but a few looked as shocked as the crowd. No one backed away. A man and a woman rushed to coffee shop man's body. When they determined that he was dead the man looked up at Baron Barnett in rage while the woman lifted the dead man's head onto her lap and sobbed loudly. Mister Henne, Awbrey remembered. The official had addressed the man lying on the ground as Mister Henne. He deserved a name. He deserved to be remembered by name.

Baron Barnett frowned at the crowd's reaction. The soldier holding Awbrey's arm spoke in a low voice. "Sir, these people won't be subdued with more killing. Perhaps the girl should wait."

"No!" Baron Barnett yelled.

Awbrey looked amongst the uniformed men for her guard. She did not know his name. Awbrey would like to know his name. She did not see him. Baron Barnett stood in front of Awbrey. He was looking at her.

Awbrey met his gaze. She could see it unfold in a few seconds. Awbrey had so little time left that what she saw when she looked into the baron's eyes was brief enough for her to comprehend what she saw. For the first time in her life Awbrey understood her talent.

When the baron put a noose around her neck the crowd would stand up to him. They were good people in this town. The only reason they had not already moved against the baron in force was a combination of politeness and confusion. They simply needed time to accept that he needed to be destroyed. Killing Mister Henne had started the process. When the baron killed her they would be stripped of all doubt and turn on him.

All those times she had looked into people's eyes and been swamped with images that only left a few lasting impressions she had been seeing the future unfold but it was too much information for her mind to absorb. The images would fade quickly, leaving her with impressions only. Sometimes the events would be so strong that she could remember vague flashes. Now that she faced only a few minutes of life left to her, there was less to see so she could remember everything she saw.

"You could have at least cleaned her first," the baron muttered to the man standing next to her when he saw the dried blood covering her.

"You said to bring her immediately," the man said.

The baron put the noose around Awbrey's neck himself. The rope was heavy and itchy. Awbrey stood with her head up and shoulders straight though fear filled every cell in her body. She looked out at the crowd of people surging against the line of uniformed men. They could not save her. Awbrey knew that they wanted to. Awbrey felt good to know that they would not stop trying even as she breathed her last breath. They would storm the uniformed men and reach Baron Barnett and he would hang on the same rope he had just put around her neck.

"You will not stop me from my destiny," the baron said as he pulled the noose snug under her chin.

"If you have a destiny then nothing will stop it. That is why it's called destiny," Awbrey said.

"I saw you in the ball. You cannot stop me," Baron Barnett said again.

Awbrey watched him step back. The urge to beg for her life came then passed. He would not spare her. To beg was futile. Knowing that begging would do no good but to feed his need for control kept her tongue still. A feeling of wild helplessness filled her. This was it.

Awbrey closed her eyes. She pushed away thoughts of Eddy lying on the grass with his life's blood pouring from his neck. Awbrey remembered when they learned that their parents had agreed to their marriage. She had felt the happiest in her life at that moment. Awbrey smiled as she remembered the happiness sweeping through her body. She was going to marry Eddy in a year, when the tulips were in bloom.

The wood beneath her feet fell away with a snap and bang. Awbrey's eyes flew open and she instinctively reached for the cold, hard rope around her neck as she dropped through the hole opened below her. The last thing she saw was the crowd overwhelming the uniformed men as they surged forward to reach the hanging platform.

Chapter Fourteen

Awbrey gasped for air. Romke frowned, crossing the room in a few quick strides. Romke took her arm and guided her to the sofa even as her mother rushed to her side. Awbrey felt cold. She shivered and tried to take a breath. She felt for the rope around her neck but there was no rope. Awbrey realized that she was looking at her mother.

"Does that mean you are dead, too?" Awbrey asked her mother, tears filling her eyes.

"Hush, dear," Stella said, stroking Awbrey's hair. "I am not dead. You are not dead."

Everything was wrong. Awbrey stared at the living room of her home. The Simpsons were there. Awbrey closed her eyes and opened them again. She was still in her home in Pindstein. Abigail Simpson took her hands and rubbed them vigorously between her own small hands. Eddy leaned over her.

"Eddy!" Awbrey whispered in awe and disbelief. Awbrey jerked her hands from Abigail's soothing and reached up to touch Eddy's face. She hesitated for a moment, not wanting to learn that it was not real. Awbrey cupped Eddy's face between her palms. He was real.

He was there. He was alive. She sobbed uncontrollably in relief.

"What is wrong with the girl?" Mr. Simpson muttered.

"Everyone was dead. Eddy. Gemma. Jaydin," Awbrey whispered. She reluctantly pulled her gaze from Eddy to look at Romke but she continued to hold her beloved's face in her hands. "Romke. Everyone but Sophie. Even me."

Romke's eyebrows rose but he remained silent. He stared thoughtfully down at Awbrey, frowning at what he was thinking about. Awbrey looked back at Eddy's face trapped between her hands. Eddy patiently stood leaning over her though he was in an awkward position.

"Can't be a nightmare. Girl was awake," Mr. Simpson said.

"Everyone was dead. Even me," Awbrey whispered. It felt so real. Being in the salon in her home was what felt unreal.

"Eddy, help her up to her room," Stella said softly. "Maybe a few minutes rest will help."

Eddy pried her hands from his face and helped her stand. Awbrey touched his smile with her fingertip, tracing his lips. "I love your smile."

Tears of relief overwhelmed her. Eddy was there. He was not dead. Her Eddy was not dead. She smiled so wide that her face hurt. Tears poured down her cheeks, running under her dress collar.

Eddy took her hand in his and kissed her fingers. "I love that you love my smile," he said. "But I don't think everyone watching us feels the same way right now."

Awbrey looked around the room, at the Simpsons, Romke's dusty clothes, at the dinner table visible in the dining hall. Jane had set the table for an elaborate dinner. Awbrey glanced down at the clothes she wore. The delicate pink brocade with tiny pearls sewn around the neckline had no blood staining it. Awbrey remembered the dress. She was reliving the betrothal dinner that had been detoured by Romke's arrival.

"Did I really not die?" Awbrey asked, reaching again to feel the nonexistent rope around her throat. "Are all of you dead? I don't understand."

"Eddy, take her upstairs. I'll be up behind you," Stella said. "Everyone else, please follow me to the table. Jane has prepared a lovely feast."

"No," Awbrey said. Some of the shock was fading and the truth was dawning. "I am all right, Mama. I am all right."

"Girl's not pregnant is she?" Mr. Simpson asked Mrs. Simpson in a stage whisper.

"Hush," Mrs. Simpson said quickly.

"Let me escort you in," Romke said, taking Awbrey's arm and placing it over his arm.

Eddy grinned and gathered his sisters against him. Awbrey shivered. It felt so strange to relive the betrothal dinner. Some things had changed but mostly it was following the same path.

"Wouldn't you like something to drink first, Romke?" Hans asked, stepping up with a beer in hand.

Romke took the beer and downed it in one long chug. He handed the mug back to Hans and wiped the foam from his moustache before walking to the dining hall with Awbrey at his side. Jane appeared with a warm, damp cloth for Awbrey to wipe her tear stained face. Awbrey could smell the unguent that Jane had applied to the cloth to relieve the swelling around her eyes. The unguent was a mix of spearmint and lavender.

Romke pulled out a chair for Awbrey then plopped onto the chair next to her. Eddy seated his sisters opposite them then walked around the table to sit next to Awbrey. Stella frowned slightly as Mr. and Mrs. Simpson stood for a moment surveying the table and open chairs then separated and each sat on either side of their daughters. Jane quietly collected the name place cards that had been ignored and no longer matched.

"Oh, my," Stella said, suddenly realizing that she had forgotten something. "I missed introductions."

"My daughter, Awbrey," Stella said, gesturing at Awbrey.

"Pleased to meet you, Romke," Awbrey said politely. Romke looked at her thoughtfully then nodded once.

"Mr. and Mrs. Simpson and their son Eddard Simpson."

The man's gaze lingered on Eddy. "Ah, to be twenty again. So much energy at that tender age. I for one had more enthusiasm than sense at your age."

"Abigail and Sonata Simpson," Stella said.

"Lovely doves," Romke said with a warm smile at the two girls.

Abigail and Sonata both smiled prettily at him.

"Our son, Russell, is away on a task. He is learning his father's business."

"Unfortunate," Romke said. "I was hoping to see the boy grown."

"Is there news from Lethbridge?" Mr. Simpson asked. "How fares the king?"

"Ah, yes, our beloved king," Romke said, the slightest edge to his voice. "I am not sure if you are aware that the king has acquired a new advisor." Romke looked around the room to gauge the reactions of his audience.

The Simpson girls had their heads together and giggled over their private conversation. Eddy was mouthing words to Awbrey. The adults watched Romke with polite interest, yet Stella's attention was clearly on Jane serving the soup. Awbrey watched the same dinner unfold, goose bumps dotting her arms.

"Is there something special about this new advisor?" Mrs. Simpson asked, leaning back as far as she could as Jane ladled soup into her bowl.

"Indeed," Romke said, taking the bread basket and tearing off a large chunk of black bread. "He is against magic. Any magical talent at all."

Mr. Simpson raised one eyebrow. "Magic?"

"Yes, magic. He is convinced that anyone practicing magic is evil," Romke said.

Eddy and Mr. Simpson exchanged glances. Awbrey had missed that small exchange the first time around. Now she knew what that meant. It was strange to think of Mr. Simpson being a magician.

"Magic," Mr. Simpson muttered. "I have heard stories, of course, but magical folk are as rare as two-headed calves. That is absurd. I am more concerned with material matters. Solid matters concern me. There are rumors that there is unrest with the Garlans."

"I have also heard rumors about Garlan," Hans said.

"Indeed," Romke said, staring thoughtfully at Mr. Simpson. "King Olind has a daughter who is reputed to be, uh, of a magical nature. Olind brought the princess along on a visit to Lethbridge a few months ago."

"Did King Eldrid's new advisor insult Princess Sophie?" Eddy asked, attention now engaged.

Romke slurped three spoonfuls of soup before answering. "Indeed. You are sharp, young man."

"What is this man's name?" Hans asked.

"Baron Barnett," Romke said. Hans frowned, exchanging glances with Stella. "Yes, I thought you would recognize the name," Romke said, noting the exchange. "Baron Barnett has become the king's new best friend."

"You know the man?" Mr. Simpson asked Hans in surprise.

"Long ago," Hans said.

"Is everyone ready for the next course?" Stella asked, rising to help Jane clear the soup bowls.

Hans stared into his soup bowl, frowning at his private thoughts. Jane pulled the nearly full soup bowl out from under his gaze and he did not even blink.

"As you thought, Baron Barnett was rude to Princess Sophie. More than rude, you might say. There were some minor incidents, er, accidents to the girl while she was at Lethbridge. Nothing could be pinned on the Baron so Eldrid defended his friend and advisor," Romke said. He paused to lovingly savor the aroma drifting up from the plate of food Jane set in front of him. "Ah, rosemary tubers. Delightful."

"A princess and a magician," Abigail said. She sighed. "How romantic."

"She would be a sorceress, not a magician," her sister, Sonata said.

"Can she turn a pony into a unicorn?" Abigail asked, face lighting up in excitement at the idea.

"Only if she's a virgin," Eddy said lightly without thinking. His cheeks turned red at his mother's steely glare. "Not that she wouldn't be. Being a princess and all. A virgin." The girls giggled when he said that.

Jane brought in the next course on a large tray and set the tray on the serving chest behind the table. Jane removed the empty tuber plates and set down the new plates filled with braised and stuffed game hens at the same time. Awbrey let Jane take her plate of rosemary tubers even though she had not finished them.

"We have wonderful news to announce," Mrs. Simpson said, stabbing her last tuber as Jane grabbed her plate and set a new plate with a hen in front of her. "Eddy, please share your news."

All eyes turned to Eddy. He grinned. "I get to apprentice with Jacksol."

"Good for you!" Stella said in delight.

Hans looked up from his plate. "That is marvelous news, boy. The man is very selective."

"And there's more," Sonata said, almost bouncing in her chair with excitement.

"The rest must wait," Mrs. Simpson said, putting her hand on the girl's arm.

"Jacksol? Of Oakport?" Romke asked. "What a great honor. Has he said which province you will be groomed for?"

Eddy shook his head. "Nothing definite."

The conversation drifted to more neutral topics for a few minutes. Even Sonata had managed to clean her bones before Jane collected that course's plates. Jane returned with flat bowls of fruit, colorful melons cut into bite sized pieces with grapes and strawberries, drizzled with honey and lime juice.

"Ah, the benefits of trade," Romke said after tasting the fresh fruit.

"What is it you do for a living, Mr. Romke?" Mrs. Simpson asked.

"Retired. And it's just Romke. No Mister," Romke said. He

chuckled. "I am past the age of great adventures."

Mrs. Simpson frowned. "You are retired from adventuring? That is what you did for a living?"

Romke chuckled again. "Aye. Pretty much. Indeed." He laughed at a private thought.

"I never heard of adventuring for a living," Mrs. Simpson said.

"That's not surprising," Romke said.

There was a dull silence for several minutes. Mrs. Simpson opened her mouth then closed it, shaking her head. Mr. Simpson tried stealing some strawberries from Sonata's plate and the girl put her arm on the table to protect her food from theft. Mrs. Simpson's attention was diverted as she scolded the girl for having her arm on the table.

"I had a dream last night," Abigail said to Awbrey. "I was in a field of flowers and the sun was shining. I could smell the flowers and it was perfect. The field was filled with bees. They hummed as they went from flower to flower. Sometimes they brushed against my hands and arms, all soft and furry and it tickled."

Awbrey stared at the girl for a minute then forced a smile. "That is a nice dream. Lots of happy, working bees means that you will be fortunate."

"There's more," Abigail said. "There was a shadow and I looked up. There was a giant baby. Tall enough to block the sun. He had a runny nose and was crying and slapping the bees."

"Marjory said it means she'll marry some poor farmer and have hordes of babies," Sonata said quickly.

"I don't even know any farmer boys," Abigail said, glaring at her younger sister.

"Marjory is wrong," Awbrey said.

"You interpret dreams?" Romke asked Awbrey.

"Everyone does," Sonata said. "It's just that Awbrey is always right."

"It's just a matter of understanding the symbols. If I am often right it is just that I know Abigail so well," Awbrey said.

The feeling of reliving the moment was uncomfortable. Everything was the same. If she had seen the future and it continued on the same course, what good was it to see what was coming and be unable to stop it?

"What if someone said reading dreams is magic?" Romke asked. Romke raised his right hand when Stella opened her mouth. It was the slightest gesture. Stella did not say anything.

Stella laughed. "No one can say my daughter is magic. Look at her. Look at her. Is that the image of evil?" Stella stood. "Excuse me. I must see what is holding up dessert."

"Perhaps we should forgo dessert," Mrs. Simpson said, staring after Stella's retreating back.

"No!" both Simpson girls protested in unison. "Besides, we still have to share the other news," Sonata added.

"Everyone already knows, Sonata," Abigail said.

"I shall assist Stella," Mrs. Simpson said, standing and walking briskly to the kitchen.

"What brings you to Pindstein, Romke?" Mr. Simpson asked.

"Just a stopover," Romke said.

"You are so quiet, Awbrey," Eddy said in a low voice. "Are you sure you are all right?"

Awbrey nodded but still did not say anything. It was so wonderful to be sitting at the table with her family that she wanted to enjoy every moment.

Stella and Mrs. Simpson returned to the table bearing trays filled with bowls of ice cream. The ice cream was filled with nuts and berries. The ice cream held everyone's attention and silence settled over the table, the only sound was of spoons tapping the porcelain bowls. Ice cream was such a special, rare treat. Jane had obviously made the treat to celebrate the agreement of Simpsons and Tiegs agreeing to allow the marriage of their children.

The dinner party moved into the salon to relax on cushioned chairs and sofas after the large meal. Awbrey and Eddy sat at the game table with game pieces sitting on the square markings before them. Awbrey stared at the game pieces but kept her hands on her lap. Eddy played with a carved dog, twirling it with his long, lean fingers.

"What do you think of Princess Sophie being magic?" Eddy asked.

"I don't know," Awbrey said, looking up at Eddy. It was all happening the same. Could she change it? What could she do to stop

Eddy from dying?

"If you were magic you would tell me wouldn't you?" Eddy asked.

"Of course. Just as you would tell me, Eddy," Awbrey said, looking into his eyes. Eddy nodded thoughtfully.

"It would be neat to talk to animals," Sonata said from below the table. "If I was magic that's what I would want to do. I wonder what a chicken would say?"

Eddy rolled his eyes. "Brat. You are sneakier than a cat. Get out from under there."

"Magic isn't evil," Sonata said, not moving from her spot under the game table. "Magic is wonderful."

"Girls, it's time to leave," Mrs. Simpson announced.

Sonata crawled out from under the table, pushing her skirt down as she stood. Awbrey looked up from the game table. Romke remained sitting on a cushioned chair, feet resting on a hassock, a mug of beer in his hand, and foam on his moustache. Mr. Simpson was already in the foyer, his hat on his head.

"Wait," Awbrey said, standing. "Since Romke is family, please announce the betrothal."

"Another time, Awbrey," Stella said.

"No. It has to be now," Awbrey said gently but firmly.

Stella stared at her daughter for a long moment. Finally she nodded her head once. "Very well. John and Laura, Hans and I welcome you to our family with the upcoming nuptials between our children."

"Stella," Laura Simpson said hesitantly, glancing at her husband.

"Stella and Hans, Laura and I welcome you to our family with the upcoming nuptials between our children," John Simpson said.

Awbrey let out her breath in relief. Eddy grinned and kissed her lightly on the lips to seal the betrothal. Romke stood and approached Awbrey and Eddy. He kissed both Eddy's cheeks. "Welcome to the family."

Everyone lined up for the ritual cheek kissing. Stella and Hans kissed Eddy's cheeks and welcomed him to the family. The Simpsons all took their turn kissing Awbrey's cheeks. Each one welcomed her to the family.

Awbrey took Eddy's hand and walked to the foyer to say good nights. She stood waiting with her parents as the Simpsons gathered together in the foyer and prepared to leave. There was the scurry to find the girls' wraps while Stella and Mrs. Simpson discussed the recipe for the ice cream. Mr. Simpson stood patiently waiting.

"Stay, Eddy," Romke said.

"Sure," Eddy said, glancing at his father. Mr. Simpson nodded.

The Tiegs and Eddy returned to the salon once the door had been shut on the departing Simpson family. Awbrey walked around the salon, picking up items, running her hands along the writing desk. Eddy hovered over her protectively, aware that something was wrong. Hans and Stella settled onto chairs, watching Awbrey with worried eyes.

"What happened, Awbrey?" Stella asked.

"I often see flashes of, well, impressions mostly," Awbrey said. She took Eddy's hand. "I look into people's eyes and I see my future related to them. Most of the time I barely remember. But this one was so real. And vivid. I thought I had lived it. Now I see that it's what's to come." Awbrey stared into nothing and shivered. Eddy rubbed his thumb on her hand soothingly. "He killed everyone but Sophie. It was horrible."

"Where did Baron Barnett kill everyone, Awbrey?" Romke asked.

"Green Falls," Awbrey said.

Romke exchanged glances with Stella and Hans. "It was a good plan, Green Falls," Romke said.

"Tell us what you saw," Hans said.

Awbrey told the tale in the perspective of having lived it, which she had in her mind. She glossed over some details, like the bickering that constantly flared. Awbrey did not gloss over the horror of the angry man attacking Romke on the side of the road. Romke turned startled eyes on Eddy when Awbrey reached the point in the story revealing Eddy's talent. Eddy looked at Romke and shrugged.

When Awbrey reached the point where Baron Barnett had everyone killed the tears flowed freely down her face. It was all still raw and vivid in her mind. Eddy put his arms around her and held her close.

"It was my fault. I couldn't ignore when he went after the children," Awbrey said, hiccupping.

"Which is why he goes after the children, to draw you out," Romke said.

"He really saw me in his crystal ball?" Awbrey asked. She shivered.

"He knew your face," Romke said, nodding.

"He doesn't see you, Romke," Eddy said.

"Eh?" Romke asked in surprise.

"He let you go in Green Falls. That means that he can't see you in his crystal ball."

"Indeed," Romke said thoughtfully. He nodded. "Indeed. That changes everything."

"If the future is defined then there's no changing what happens," Awbrey said.

"Did we have this discussion before, Awbrey?" Romke asked. Awbrey shook her head. "Then it's already changed," Romke pointed out.

"You must return to Lethbridge," Hans said to Romke. "He will not see you coming."

"Can you destroy the crystal ball?" Romke asked Eddy. Eddy hesitated then nodded. Romke stood. "Do it. For all we know he followed the crystal ball."

"He was right there," Awbrey said.

"But Eddy had hidden it," Romke said.

"It's changed," Hans said. "Already it's changed."

"It's up to me then. You need to take the children with you in case I fail. But you stand a chance now. The future is unknown to the baron."

"How do you know he didn't already see this?" Awbrey asked.

"He is not looking for me," Romke said. "That either means I fail or the future has changed. Either way, we stand a better chance if we don't go to Green Falls. That outcome we know."

"That is still the route he will take," Hans said. He stood. "I will take the wagon to Green Falls. Everyone else must stay here. Except Romke. Romke must go back to Lethbridge. It is the only way it will work."

"How do you know?" Awbrey asked.

Hans smiled. "I know the baron. He will go to Green Falls and stay the course."

"Then why is Romke going to Lethbridge?" Eddy asked.

"To stop the baron and convince the king to rescind the new law," Romke said.

Awbrey stared at her father. "You helped me see the whole thing, didn't you? Father?"

Hans nodded. "I suspected what was happening and I held you in the vision. I am sorry that it was such a painful experience. It was an opportunity. I get glimpses but that is all. I am sorry, Awbrey. I thought it would be good to see what unfolded so I held you in the vision."

Awbrey stood and hugged her father. "Thank you. You saved us. All of us."

"It isn't over yet, Awbrey," Eddy warned.

"But it won't be the same, Eddy," Awbrey said. "Maybe you should go with Romke to Lethbridge?"

Eddy stared at her. "You want me to assassinate the man in cold blood."

"He killed you, Eddy," Awbrey said. "He killed me. He killed children." Awbrey turned to her father. "Can you help him see what happened?"

"It's not necessary," Eddy said. "I will go to Lethbridge with Romke."

Hans physically relaxed. "Your father as well. He will go. The three of you will succeed."

Awbrey walked Eddy and Romke to the foyer. Most of the memories were already fading. The horror of Eddy being killed seemed farther away than that same day. Eddy would go to Lethbridge with Romke and stop the baron. They would be safe. They would get married in the spring when the tulips were in bloom.

# # #

www.ingramcontent.com/pod-product-compliance
Lightning Source LLC
Chambersburg PA
CBHW070911180626
46817CB00003B/1018